NURSE
IN
CHARGE

NURSE IN CHARGE

Jane Converse

Thorndike Press • Chivers Press
Thorndike, Maine USA   Bath, England

This Large Print edition is published by Thorndike Press, USA and by Chivers Press, England.

Published in 2000 in the U.S. by arrangement with Maureen Moran Agency.

Published in 2000 in the U.K. by arrangement with the author.

U.S. Hardcover 0-7862-2860-1   (Candlelight Series Edition)
U.K. Hardcover 0-7540-4377-0   (Chivers Large Print)

Roy
1070796

The text of this Large Print edition is unabridged.
Other aspects of the book may vary from the original edition.

Set in 16 pt. Plantin by Anne Bradeen.

Printed in the United States on permanent paper.

British Library Cataloguing-in-Publication Data available

Library of Congress Cataloging-in-Publication Data

Converse, Jane.
    Nurse in charge / by Jane Converse.
        p. cm.
    ISBN 0-7862-2860-1 (lg. print : hc : alk. paper)
    1. Nurses — Fiction. 2. Large type books. I. Title.
PS3553.O544 N875 2000
    813'.54—dc21   00-059378

NURSE
IN
CHARGE

One

Kitty Simmons settled back in one of the old wicker chairs dotting Doc Osgood's reception room, a nostalgic smile crossing her face as she surveyed the familiar, shabby surroundings.

Nothing had changed, she noticed. There was Doc's framed graduation certificate, dated June 18, 1919. There was the same ugly brown glazed pot holding the same scraggly fern that had fascinated her when she paid visits to Doc's office as a child. Those tattered comic books were of more recent vintage, but the monstrous round oak dining-room table that held them still wobbled on its legs. Years ago, Doc had sawed them down, making the table accessible to his smaller patients. In the old days, a thickness of pillbox cardboard had been wedged under the short leg. It was gone now. Doc needed help, all right. Someone to attend to details like this.

Kitty listened for a moment to the muffled sound of Doc's voice from one of the examining rooms down the hall. The words were unintelligible, but the brusque, booming quality of that voice broadened her smile. She had been afraid that the years had slowed Doc's pace. As long as he could still bellow like a walrus, there was no need to worry.

Restless, eager to see the old man's expression when he found her waiting for him, Kitty got up to cross the little room. From its single wide window, she could see almost the whole of Main Street. She had walked past all those drab buildings and shops a few moments earlier, going from the bus stop which doubled as the Eldridge Emporium (Dry Goods, Housewares, and Sundries) to cross in front of the grocery store-post office, then the barber shop, and, finally, the decrepit frame two-story hotel where she had taken a room, freshened up after the long ride from Minneapolis, and left her luggage. A black-and-gold, wind-battered sign still hung from the hotel's upper porch rail, reading: "THE RITZ. Finest Accommodations in Eldridge, South Dakota. Population 837. Watch us Grow!"

Eldridge had chosen to do nothing of the kind; the sign had been hanging there back when Kitty had attended the elementary school around the corner on Grant Street, and the town's population was still frozen under the thousand mark. Nor had Aunt Emma's Café, which occupied most of the hotel's first floor, found it necessary to add to its ten counter stools and four tables.

There were no other landmarks to detain tourists who drove through Eldridge on their way to fishing and hunting lodges north of the town. Not unless you counted the Community Church and an adjoining wooden building that served as the town's meeting hall and "cultural center." When the church coffers ran low, the Ladies Aid sometimes rented an old movie to show there, and Eldridge's youth occasionally gathered in the drafty building to dance to records. During the day, old men gathered in its rooms to play checkers. Strange, the way you could admit that it wasn't much of a town; yet coming back after four years of living in an interesting city was a thrill, because Eldridge was, after all, home. Only Mom's absence detracted from Kitty's joy; she was conspicuously missing inside this old red brick building that everyone called Doc Osgood's "hospital." And the romantic prospects weren't too promising. Still, maybe there would be someone who. . . .

A door opened at the end of the corridor,

and Doc's voice reverberated from the walls. "If you'd listened to me, Sonny, you could have saved us both a lot of bother. Damn lucky you didn't blow off your fool leg. What d'you think guns are *for*, anyway? Got one purpose — and that's to maim or kill. I tell you, I'm pretty doggone sick of patchin' up idiots who think a gun's got some other use."

Doc hadn't changed his tune, Kitty reflected. A naturalist and a dedicated enemy of violence, he carried on a continuing battle with even the closest of his cronies, all of whom were hunters in this hunters' paradise.

As he drew nearer, accompanying a patient whose footsteps indicated a limp, Doc's tone softened. "Okay, Sonny. Let's get the dressing changed again, and let me have another look at you tomorrow."

Kitty heard a hesitant, boyish voice asking, "Ma said to ask if it's all right if . . . ?"

"You tell her she's all square with me," Doc roared. "Two apple pies and all that grape jelly? By golly, you tell your ma she's paid up enough so's you can blow off your *left* toe if you're still itchin' to fool around with a damn rifle. Get outta here, now. I got Miz Jorgensen comin' in with her bursitis — Miz Vitelli think-in' she's havin' labor pains,

10

but not sure it's not just the pickled pigs feet and sauerkraut she ate last night. I got so much to do since I lost that wonderful nurse, I don't know. . . ."

Doc stopped short. His ponderous frame had emerged from the hallway, barely obscured by the small body of a sheepish teenager who preceded him on crutches. The boy's freshly bandaged foot slowed his pace, but he hobbled toward the door as quickly as possible, his head lowered so that he did not see Kitty. Nor did he turn around as Doc exclaimed, "Well, I'll be damned! Kitty Simmons! By golly, if I was a drinkin' man, I'd swear I'm seein' things and take the pledge!"

That scraggly face with its big, florid features that had been assembled with all the finesse of a lumber pile! The saucer-shaped blue eyes, childishly innocent, yet capable of dominating a room! The halo of feathery white hair around Doc's bald sun-reddened dome, and the bulging barrel of a figure still squeezed into the same old blue serge suit! The suit was Doc's concession to professional dignity, as was the black string tie. But he wore the shiny double-breasted relic with a red plaid shirt, as always, thereby declaring his independence from conformity. He was a beautiful sight, and as Doc ex-

11

tended his hamlike hands, Kitty ran to grasp them. In the next instant she was being squeezed in a bear hug that left her gasping for air.

When the old man released her, they were both laughing and on the verge of tears. "I wanted to surprise you," Kitty puffed. "I was going to write, but I. . . ."

"Decided to give me the shock of my life, eh?" Doc chuckled. "That you did, girl. That you did."

The young patient had closed the door behind him, and Doc sank his considerable weight into one of the wicker chairs, gesturing for Kitty to sit down opposite him. "Tell me how it's going girl! You like your job? How long you got to visit?"

"I'm not visiting," Kitty told him. "I'm here to stay."

Doc's eyes expressed disbelief. "*Live* here? Pretty young thing like you, with a good job in a fancy new hospital. . . ."

"I thought maybe you'd hire me, Doc. The Danielsons wrote that you need help since. . . ." Kitty hesitated, reluctant to stir up a tragic memory. Her mother hadn't had an R.N. degree, but she had worked for Doc as a practical nurse since Kitty's father had died, leaving her with a two-year-old to support. "Anyway, I figured you could use a nurse."

"Times I think I could use ten," Doc sighed. A streak of spring sunlight from the window crossed his face, and Kitty drew a quick breath, noticing for the first time that time and a gruelling schedule had taken their toll. He had always been "Old Doc" to her, but the hearty manner and bustling energy had made the word "old" a mere figure of speech. Now it was sadly accurate.

Always perceptive, Doc had read her expression. "Well, I'm pushin' seventy-two," he said. There was no self-pity in his voice; it was a flat, honest statement. "No use pretendin' I'm a spry young blade. And I've got to admit, I miss Martha for selfish reasons, too. Apart from . . . wishin' there had been something I could do for her."

Kitty nodded, the atmosphere in the room suddenly solemn. "I know you tried, Doc."

"Cancer doesn't choose between the good and the bad," Doc said quietly. "One thing you can remember, Kitty. Your ma wanted you to get your degree . . . wanted it so bad that she wouldn't let me write to you, even after we both knew there wasn't any hope. She was afraid . . . well, we *both* knew what you'd do if you were told the truth. You'd have packed up and come home."

"Sure."

"And missed out on graduating last year. Broken Martha's heart. As it was, you were a *nurse* when I finally couldn't keep it from you any longer. You got to be with your ma those last few weeks. By golly, all I could do was keep her out of pain, but you . . . wearin' that cap and uniform for Martha to see . . . you helped her die happy." Doc pulled a red bandana handkerchief from his vest pocket, blew into it, and then pretended that there was something in his eye. "Damn dust in this town," he grunted.

Kitty changed the subject hastily, her own eyes moist. "I liked working at General after I left here. Great experience. Every kind of case you can imagine, Doc. Even hunters who shot themselves in the legs. I figured I'd need to know how to take care of those if I ever wanted to come back here."

Doc managed a weak laugh, though even his less hearty laughter shook the framed diploma above his head. "Yes, by golly, that's a specialty for you! Diggin' bullets out of bunions." He shook his big head in a disparaging way, then stared at Kitty with a puzzled expression on his face. "I don't know, Kitty girl. I just don't know."

"Don't know what?"

"About you. You've been working in one of those chrome-plated hospitals, where everything goes like clockwork. This place. . . ." (Doc waved his huge arm to indicate the whole building.) "This place suits me fine, and it suits the folks here in town. 'Least I don't get too many complaints. What I wonder is . . . how's a nurse trained in one of those super efficient factories going to take to the way I run this whole shebang here?"

"You cure people when they're sick, don't you?"

Doc grinned. "Them as survive the treatment. That's what my old buddie Olie Jensen always says."

"All right, you do as well as any doctor can," Kitty argued. "I know you read. You keep up with new developments in medicine. You'll go halfway to Kingdom Come in a blizzard if someone's sick. And you *talk* to people. Do you know how important that is, when old people are sick? To have a doctor take time to listen to their complaints? Most city doctors don't have the time."

"Won't *take* time," Doc said. His eyes beamed with pride. "But don't get the idea I mollycoddle folks that're enjoyin' being sick. Got no time for hypochondriacs. Just as soon boot 'em out as give 'em the time of day."

"I know that. The people here know it,

too, and they respect you for it, Doc. They see through all your bluff, too."

Doc started to protest, evidently thought better of it, and saved his cherished reputation as a crusty, unsentimental old character, by announcing, "I give 'em hell when they deserve it. By golly, I don't care if they own the Eldridge bank. If they don't take care of themselves, I lay into 'em."

"That's because you love them," Kitty said.

Doc made a snorting sound. "Can't afford to lose too many patients. Not that many people around. Besides, I delivered just about everybody under fifty. You bring a kid through measles, mumps, chicken pox, couple of falls out of apple trees, and a clout on the nose with a baseball bat — well, you got a lot of *time* invested in him. Makes you hoppin' mad when he comes in here with a shotgun wound in his foot. It's like he didn't respect all the work you put in. Fiddlin' with a gun! Guns are an insult to my profession."

Kitty had listened to the tirade many times before, but she nodded her agreement as though she were hearing it for the first time.

Doc lumbered to his feet. "Besides, I can't promise you any regular hours, like you have in a big hospital. Work starts when

16

the first patient comes in. Quits when the last patient leaves. If we've got people here overnight, there's liable to be no time off at all."

"Do you still live upstairs?"

Doc bristled. "Anything wrong with my digs upstairs?"

Kitty suppressed a laugh. Doc's quarters, as she remembered them, were a clutter of books, stuffed squirrels, seashells, fossils, arrowheads, old *National Geographics*, a skeleton, several microscopes, framed photographs of animals, dried seed pods . . . an unbelievable collection that couldn't be organized or dusted because Doc considered every item too priceless to trust to his cleaning lady's touch.

"Mighty handy, just having to walk down the steps when I've got overnight patients," Doc was saying. "Get all my meals at Aunt Emma's, just down the block. She sends meals up when folks are hospitalized. Can't beat that for a good arrangement. Better than having some busybody housekeeper hounding me all day."

Kitty could only agree again. This was Doc's *way;* no one in Eldridge would have dreamed of suggesting a change.

He had bent over to pick a cricket from the floor, no small effort, considering his thick midsection. Dropping the insect into the fern pot as gently as he would have probed a pain-wracked abdomen, Doc said, "This is what I mean. Bet you don't have crickets up at your hospital. Jerry *lives* in this pot. Might have a hard time adjusting to the way I do things."

Kitty got up from her chair, crossing to a scarred rolltop desk. The cover was permanently drawn back to reveal a mound of papers, books, sample medications, and items too varied to classify. "I could start out straightening up this mess, Doc."

"You do, and I'll never find anything!" Doc roared. Grudgingly, he admitted that his account books could "stand being looked at." "It's not that I can't keep the books in my head," he insisted. "It's the damned government people. They came snoopin' around last May, tellin' me my income tax forms didn't make sense. I told 'em I'm a doctor, not any fool accountant, and if they want to toss me in the pokey because I'm takin' Mr. Pauley's arthritis treatment out in chickens — he sends one over to Emma every Friday and she fries it up for me — well, I said, that's fine with me, but it's too bad the government's got no more important thing to do than go mindin' somebody else's business."

Doc chuckled, remembering the incident, and Kitty had a brief vision of the tax man trying to figure out Uncle Sam's percentage of a payment that included a loaf of sourdough bread and a jar of gooseberry preserves. Wealthy people like Olie Jensen, though he was one of Doc's best friends, were charged astronomical fees for Doc's services. Old Nettie Craig, the town's acknowledged social leader — whose deceased husband had made a fortune in copper mining — had sputtered and fumed over Doc's bill after he had pulled her chauffeur through a bout with pneumonia. But the bills were always paid. And the others, the people who scrounged a living from a few rocky acres outside of town, gave Doc what they had to give . . . and that was sometimes nothing at all.

"I don't want anybody changing things," Doc warned.

"I wouldn't think of it," Kitty promised.

Doc looked dubious. "Sure you will. You're young. Pretty. Even if you get used to this place, you'll be wantin' to meet. . . ." He shrugged his massive shoulders. "Let's just say this town isn't overcrowded with marriage-minded young men. Girl's had an education like yours, that cuts down the eligibles even more. You won't stay, Kitty.

Better think twice before you burn your bridges back in Minneapolis."

"They're fried to a crisp," Kitty said.

"Your job?"

"I've quit that."

Doc scowled. "Young men?"

"I didn't leave any broken hearts behind me, Doc. Just about every male worth having at the hospital was married. I had dates, but. . . ." It was Kitty's turn to shrug. "Nobody special. I guess I just got home-sick, that's all."

"Doesn't make sense," Doc said. He was peering out the window. "Here comes my bursitis gal."

"Doc, will you please tell me if I'm hired or fired or . . . ?"

"No sense at all," he went on, as though Kitty weren't in the room. "Well, maybe it does. Freckles all over your nose. Dishwater blond hair. Walk like a tomboy — short — figure could stand a little fillin' out. Nose turns up, mouth's too big." Doc was standing with his head cocked to one side, faking a disapproving expression as he surveyed Kitty. "Those big blue eyes aren't enough to make up for all the bad features. Yes, I can see where the boys would pass you by. Not much to look at, are you?"

It had taken Kitty several seconds to realize that he was teasing her . . . the way he had teased when she had been ill with the mumps at the age of seven — miserable, but breaking up with giggles at Doc's whimsical bedside manner. He was a lot older now, his funny face lined with deep creases, but he was remembering, too. "By golly, if you don't look like a chipmunk with pigtails. Maybe some old farmer who can't do any better will feel sorry for you and offer to let you get hitched up to him. Poor little thing!"

Kitty's eyes welled with tears. "Oh, Doc . . . that's exactly what you said to me when. . . ."

"I know. I know!" The big hands (so delicate in removing a bullet or replacing a cricket!) . . . Doc's huge hands were patting Kitty's shoulder. "You *did* look like a chipmunk with jowls full of acorns. But . . . maybe you're a shade better-looking now. I don't know that I'd mind having you around . . . my Christian duty to be kind to the less fortunate. Homely girls have a tough row to hoe."

His eyes were laughing, telling Kitty she was lovely and that he couldn't understand why she would want to bury herself in an unorthodox "hospital" in a dreary town like Eldridge. But his expression was also telling her that she was loved and that she was needed and that there was no way for a rough old country doctor to tell her that he was grateful for her offer of help. Because he *was* tired; no amount of joking or bellowing or stamping around like a bull elephant could disguise the fact that Doc Osgood was weary from a lifetime of service to this community. He was "pushing seventy-two," and he probably hadn't slept more than five hours in a row in the past forty-five years. "Okay, since you can't find work anywhere else, I'll pay you what you're worth," he barked suddenly. "Don't blame me if I give you a bill at the end of the week. Start right now if you want to."

Someone was coming up the brick steps outside. "Mrs. Jorgensen," Kitty said with exaggerated efficiency. "Bursitis. Where would I find her card?"

Doc waved at the rolltop desk. "In there, somewhere. Where would you *expect* to find it? And don't forget to collect as she goes out. Miz Jorgensen's a cash customer. Got money in her mattress must have been printed by Adam, and you've got to remind that type."

Doc had pounded back to one of the examining rooms, and Kitty was plowing through the litter of papers inside the

rolltop desk when their patient walked in —
a dour, dyspeptic woman who looked at
Kitty with only mild surprise before she
asked, "Aren't you Martha Simmons' girl? I
thought you'd gone off to the city."

"I came back," Kitty told her. She felt a
rush of gladness; a joyous sensation of being
at home, where she belonged. "If you'll just
make yourself comfortable, Mrs. Jorgensen,
Doc will see you in a minute."

Two

Whenever Kitty had thought of returning to
Eldridge, she had assumed that she would
again occupy the small frame cottage in
which she had spent her childhood. Although
it belonged to Kitty now, it was rented to a
young, newly married couple, and Kitty
abandoned the idea of asking them to move
when she walked past the house during her
first week in town. Choking up at the sight of
a privet hedge her mother had planted, depressed by the recollection of her last visit to
the house, Kitty knew that she could never
live there again. Instead of knocking on the
door, she walked on, closing a door on the
past.

There were offers of room and board from
a number of people, among them George
and Erma Danielson, who owned the drugstore and had been Martha Simmons'
closest friends. Kitty expressed her thanks
but chose to remain in what was whimsically
called "the Presidential Suite" at The Ritz,

following Doc's routine of eating her meals at Aunt Emma's.

There were practical reasons, too, for Kitty's decision. Doc Osgood had not exaggerated when he had told her that hours at his hospital were not dictated by the clock but by the needs of his patients. Living less than a block away from the austere brick building in which she worked, Kitty was available at whatever odd hour of the day or night Doc required her help. Once, keeping constant vigil over an elderly, excitable coronary patient, Kitty stayed at the hospital for three nights in succession, insisting that Doc go upstairs to get his rest and taking catnaps on the worn leather sofa in his office when the patient slept.

There were quiet days when everyone in Eldridge was apparently in good health and uninjured. But there were days when the variety of ailments with which people could become inflicted seemed inexhaustible. Perversely, the deluge of patients seemed to come on the days that Doc drove his antiquated Chevy pickup — which also served as the town's ambulance — to West Fork, a larger community some forty miles south of Eldridge, to perform elective surgery in that town's better equipped and staffed hospital. More often than not, Kitty found herself performing duties that were properly reserved for M.D.'s. She was doing more than learning; she was fulfilling the highest potential of a nurse, and more.

As the druggist's wife expressed it when Kitty stopped at the soda fountain for a Coke one evening, "It takes a very special person to hold down your job, Kitty. You have to be able to see through all of Doc's blustering. Tolerate all his eccentric ways. And live with that harum-scarum practice of his. My goodness, how many nurses trained in a modern hospital would do what you do? And *like* it!"

"Don't let the chaos that you see on the surface fool you," Kitty warned. "Doc's hospital may seem a little disorganized, but his patients get the kind of medical services I can respect. I've given up trying to straighten out Doc's books. . . ."

Mrs. Danielson laughed. "I wasn't even sure he kept a record of his accounts."

"Just the same, when I get back to my room after a day's work, I feel . . . I guess the word is 'fulfilled.' "

"Professionally, you mean."

"Yes."

Plump and motherly, Erma Danielson examined Kitty with a questioning look. "There's more to living in a town than liking your job, dear. You haven't been having any good times. One dinner with old fuddy-duddies like George and me. I was thinking . . . you haven't met Vernon Olwyler, have you?"

"The name doesn't ring a bell."

"Vern's new here. He came to take over the elementary school when Mrs. Lawford retired last February. Young bachelor. *Very* pleasant man." Kitty could almost see the matchmaking wheels spinning inside the older woman's head. "We'll have to have the two of you over for dinner one night soon. If we can drag you away from Doc's place, that is. Next thing we know, Doc will be retiring and you'll be in full charge."

Erma Danielson, along with Kitty, had smiled at the facetious remark. But it turned out to be prophetic, and the meeting with the town's most eligible bachelor was post-poned indefinitely.

Change came to Doc's hospital swiftly and unexpectedly one morning, in the form of a fourteen-year-old boy from a nearby farm. Doc had just returned from a remote cabin in Box Canyon, thirty miles distant, after delivering a baby. Puffing with exhaustion and haggard from loss of sleep (for he had been called out shortly after four that morning), Doc came into his office at al-

27

most the same moment that Petey McLellan was carried in by an elderly uncle and an older brother. Blood-soaked and moaning with pain, the boy was fully conscious as his terrified relatives followed Kitty's directions and eased him, face down, onto an examining table. His shirt and trousers had been pulled back to reveal a deep, ugly gash across his lower back.

"Thank God you're here," Kitty whispered.

Doc took one look at the wound, gave Kitty orders for a hypo that would render the boy mercifully unaware, and — under his breath — said, as Doc *always* said whenever an emergency case confronted him, "We're going to have to move fast, girl."

He was scrubbing at the corner sink, and Kitty was cutting the patient's clothing away, when Doc barked, "What happened?"

The boy's brother was almost in tears. "We was tryin' to get this old tiller workin'. The motor. Pete was up on top, and, all of a sudden, the motor kicked over. I guess he got jerked outta his seat. Next thing I know, he's screamin' — hooked on one of them rusty blades. We had to . . . get him off. . . ."

Kitty let an inward shudder run through her. She had, in Doc's rough parlance, "knocked the patient out," and, without being told to do so, was preparing the grit and blood crusted field for debridement. Moving quickly, automatically, she reached for gauze pads and antiseptic liquid soap — thinking ahead, anticipating Doc's need for sterile instruments from the autoclave.

"Going to have to cut away all that torn flesh," Doc was saying, unnecessarily. "Get all that barnyard gook out of there. You . . . Willie . . . you and your uncle better go wait outside. We've got enough to do without somebody passin' out cold."

Kitty's fleeting glance at the patient's relatives confirmed Doc's concern; they were both so pale and shaken that the mere sight of a scalpel would have sent them into a faint.

At the door, the overalls-clad older man hesitated.

"Doc, are you sure you can . . . ?" His voice broke. "If somethin' should happen to my sister's boy . . . you know she lost Jim last year. . . ."

"If you didn't think I could do something for Pete, you wouldn't have brought him here!" Doc snapped. He turned from the scrub sink, shaking his hands dry. In another second he would perform the near-impossible feat of pulling on his sterile gloves without help; Doc had learned a few tricks, operating as a loner. "Go on! Git! Kitty and I have work to do!"

For an instant, Kitty was angered by Doc's harshness. Couldn't he see that the McLellans had just gone through a horrible experience, that they were frightened and helpless? A sympathetic word of reassurance. . . .

Then, as she began washing the field of operation, Kitty realized that any change from Doc's normal brusque manner would have made the ordeal twice as excruciating for the two men. They knew Doc, and Doc knew them. Soft-spoken commiseration would have told them that nothing could be done to save the boy. By being his usual tough and outspoken self, Doc had conveyed the message that he was his old *confident* self. The McLellans left the room knowing that God was in His Heaven, Doc was in his hospital, and, somehow, all would be well again.

I should know this about him, Kitty thought. Draping the field, she remembered the only time she had ever heard Doc speak gently to a patient's next of kin. He had spoken to her, and he had said, "I'm sorry, Kitty. I've done all I could, and there's no more a doctor can do."

Doc had been beaten by an incurable illness then. He was far from helpless now. A sign of his confidence was the casual way in which he began to talk, as his big hands started the delicate task of cutting away the mangled, contaminated tissue. "Petey's one of my kids, you know. Just like you, Kitty. I delivered all the McLellan youngsters — and their ma, too. How d'you like that?"

Whenever Doc tackled a sensitive job he kept a steady stream of words going — sometimes only muttering trivialities to himself, sometimes expounding in a loud voice on a totally unrelated subject. He reminded Kitty of a surgeon in Minneapolis who had shocked her by telling risqué stories during the most critical operations. She had thought him profane and indifferent until she recognized the jokes as a safety valve for an almost unimaginable pressure. Doc kept his tension under control with idle chatter. Certainly, if you watched his eyes and his hands, you knew that every ounce of his attention was concentrated on the job he was doing.

"Rust, barnyard manure, and damp soil," he was saying now. "There's a made-to-order combination for tetanus. Now, you see the advantage of knowing your patients from the second they're born? We'll give Petey a booster when we're finished patching him up. But a booster's no more than water in the veins if your patient hasn't had those basic shots. I gave them to this laddie myself, so I *know*." Doc dropped a scalpel to the floor and selected another. "Wish we'd had time to get you boiled, Kitty." ("Boiled" was Doc's term for asepsis; there had been no time for Kitty to scrub.) "I'd get spoiled, though, with half a dozen assistants handing me sponges and holding retractors. Down at the big hospital in West Fork they've got people falling all over each other. Anaesthetists, nurses, doctors . . . by golly, did I ever tell you about the time Henry Purcell brought his wife in here with a ruptured appendix? I was here all by my lonesome and if you've ever seen a man, *move*, you should have. . . ."

Kitty had been standing aside, washing her hands in a small basin she had filled with Phisohex, at the same time watching the patient for signs of shock. As Doc's speech was cut off abruptly, Kitty looked up to see if there was something he needed. Glancing at his face, Kitty tensed. His complexion was gray, and his forehead was wet with perspiration. More shocking was the trembling of Doc's hands; he was barely able to hold onto the scalpel! Kitty moved forward. "Doc? What's wrong?"

He was swaying dizzily, fighting to catch his breath. "I can't finish," Doc gasped. "Kitty . . . take over. Quick!"

A coronary? The words flashed through Kitty's mind, leaving her numb for a terrible instant. Then, reaching out with the thought of guiding him to a chair, Kitty recoiled as he bellowed, *"I said . . . take over!"*

"But you. . . ."

"Never mind . . . me. Patient on the table. Finish!"

Kitty's eyes fell to the grisly operation that Doc had started. She had never before used a scalpel: The thought of cutting too deeply, touching a vital nerve — an artery. . . .

"You can . . . do it!" Doc panted. He had let the knife fall from his shaking fingers and was gripping the edge of the table for support. Mouthing the words with difficulty, Doc emphasized, "You've . . . *got* to do it, Kitty. I'll . . . tell you what . . . to do."

"You can't stay on your feet," Kitty pleaded. "Doc, you've got to. . . ."

"Do as I say!" he ordered. It was a sobbing cry, but it was a furious command, too.

Kitty reached into the autoclave for a sterile knife. Her own hands were only a trifle more steady than Doc's. He noticed that and lowered his voice, softening his tone but keeping it firm. "You aren't in any . . . danger zone, girl. Common sense. You're cleaning. Plenty of gauze pads ready. You're fine. Easy. Remember . . . it's no different than . . . cleaning an abrasion . . . get that grimy edge out of the way. Can't leave any dirt inside . . . clean . . . get it clean."

He kept holding onto the table, breathing heavily, but never stopping the reassuring words, never taking his gaze from the field of operation. And Kitty, with her teeth biting into her lower lip, obeyed, never daring to look up at Doc, only vaguely aware that he had moved back a few inches so that the icy perspiration pouring across his face would not drop down to contaminate the wound. She didn't dare think of what she would do if Doc collapsed, if the calm, encouraging instructions came to an end. Instinct told her that Doc would hang on until their job was completed: Doc would manage because he *had* to. Was it knowing that Doc would remain at her side that accomplished the miracle? Kitty's hands guided the scalpel steadily and swiftly, as though she had been debriding tissue all of her life. And, somehow, she was holding a needle and hearing Doc saying, "Small bites. That's it. Nice, clean suture. You've seen it done a . . . thousand times. Good. Another small bite. That's my girl.

Fine. Fine. Good, clean closure."

He wouldn't have had to stay to watch Kitty apply the dressing or to see that the boy was given the vital booster shot, but Doc did. It was only when Pete McLellan's brother and uncle were called in to move him to a hospital bed across the hall that Kitty was able to turn her attention to the old man.

"He's . . . going to be fine," Doc puffed. "Good girl. Good girl."

Kitty placed an arm under Doc's. "Let me get the men to help you. Oh, Doc . . . tell me what's wrong? What . . . ?"

"I'm all right. Get to my . . . couch in the office . . . walk myself . . . don't worry."

He did so, with Kitty feeling superfluous at his side, knowing that she could not support Doc's weight if his legs buckled under him, but also knowing better than to argue with him and risk any excitement.

When he dropped down to the old black leather sofa, Doc released a long sigh, closed his eyes, and said, "It's not my heart, if . . . that's what's worrying you, girl. No pain. Just . . . giving out. You know? Perfectly sound machine . . . parts start to wear out. Been . . . driving 'er too hard."

"Tell me what I can do for you," Kitty said gently.

"Let me . . . rest for a bit. See to the boy.

After a while . . . come back, Kitty. We've got some . . . talkin' to do."

Doc was an excellent diagnostician; if he said that his problem was old age and exhaustion, it was probably true. Kitty covered him with a light blanket, swabbed his face with a cool moist towel, and let him rest.

Crossing the hall to check on her emergency patient, Kitty was stricken with a violent case of what Doc called "the post-op jitters." If *he* was sometimes affected, this delayed reaction was to be expected in her own case, Kitty thought. She had performed *surgery!* If the patient on the table had required the incision of an organ, Doc would have done exactly what he did today. He would have said "take over . . . finish" and expected Kitty to follow through.

It had been an awesome experience. It was even more so when Petey, regaining consciousness to find himself surrounded by grateful relatives and an even more grateful nurse, groaned, "Last time I was here, I got ice cream." There was subdued laughter, and there were a few tears to blink back, knowing that the boy would leave Doc's hospital soon and that he would have only a clean scar on his back to show for his near-tragic experience.

"Pete had his tonsils snipped last time," the boy's uncle explained. "I guess he gave Doc a little more trouble today."

Kitty nodded. "He's a lucky boy. It could have been worse."

"We're all lucky," the older McLellan boy said huskily. "I mean, havin' this hospital, and all." He was looking at his brother's tranquil face as he added, "I sure don't know what we'd do around here without Doc."

They would never be told, of course, that Doc had already given more than he was able to give to this community. Kitty used her own discretion in selecting a sedative that would give Pete several more pain-free hours of sleep while he recovered from his ordeal. When she left the sleeping boy in his mother's care later, she was not nearly as concerned about the patient's well-being as that of his doctor — the beloved, respected, indispensable doctor who had asked her to come back to his office later because they had "some talking to do." She could smile with satisfaction, looking at Pete. Knowing what Doc was going to tell her made it hard to hold back tears.

Three

"Keep writing it down the way I tell you," Doc ordered. "And I don't want any more sniffling and back talk from you, young lady. Now, where were we?"

Seated across from the couch on which Doc had reclined his ponderous body, Kitty blinked back her tears and gave her attention to the scribbled notes she had been taking. " 'This practice is available free of charge only to a Capital D Doctor who is more interested in curing patients than fattening his bank account,' " Kitty read aloud. "Namby-pambies will not survive. A qualified and dedicated M.D. will be primarily rewarded in nonnegotiable assets, such as the respect and devotion of this community. Clock watchers need not apply."

Kitty looked up from the note pad, frowning. "Doc, isn't this a little . . . ?"

"Strong? I *want* it strong!" Doc roared. "Separate the doctors from the dilettantes beforehand."

"I was thinking . . . the copy might be a bit undignified for a professional journal."

"I'm paying for the ad. Say exactly what I've got to say. By golly, it's honest, isn't it?"

It was *too* honest, Kitty thought. Although Doc's offer of turning his practice over to a young medic with no money involved was unbelievably generous, he had dictated a masterpiece of eccentricity that would probably scare off more prospects than it would attract. Kitty could not recall a young doctor in her acquaintance who wouldn't laugh off the statement that read, "House calls involve 30-plus miles of driving through snow in winter, mud in fall and spring, dust in summer."

As delicately as possible, Kitty suggested that perhaps the ad could be trimmed down. "At a dollar a word, you're running up quite a bill here," she suggested. "Couldn't you just . . . give the bare facts and have anyone who's interested write for details?"

"Don't have time for a lot of correspondence," Doc grumbled. "Did you get the point about top recommendations? We don't want some bumbling idiot who squeaked through med school at the bottom of his class and can't find a berth anywhere else. Don't want anybody using my people for pin cushions 'cause he can't find a vein."

"It's all here." Kitty patted the notebook and got up from her chair. "I just wish. . . ."

"You just wish I didn't have to face facts," Doc snapped. "Now, you look here, Kitty. Long ago I promised myself that when I'm no longer able to give my patients the best possible care . . . the very *best* possible care . . . I'd quit. The time is here, and I'm not going to go around blubbering about it. I'd feel a lot worse if there wasn't anybody here to take over this place. Now that *would* be a reason for being miserable."

Kitty paused on her way to the little cubicle where Doc kept a dilapidated old typewriter. "It's going to be so strange, having someone else in charge."

"I'll be around," Doc promised. "Upstairs, busy with my bugs and butterflies and whatnot. You won't get rid of me that easily, you and your new boss."

Kitty nodded and left the room to type the ad, along with two almost identical letters that Doc had addressed to former colleagues in other states, asking them to "scout around and see if you can flush out an exceptional young M.D.; up on modern techniques but with a horse-and-buggy dedication."

It was late in June, and Doc had started

sending his more seriously ill patients to the hospital in West Fork, before he received the one and only response to his call for a replacement. In the usual informal style of Eldridge's hospital, there were three extra people present when Doc read the letter aloud to Kitty. It was a concise, formal letter, describing the doctor's training, internship, and residency. He would complete his last year as a resident in a major Chicago hospital at the end of the month, and his written recommendations, which were enclosed, were of the highest quality. A varied and challenging practice were prime considerations, the writer concluded, and monetary rewards were secondary.

"By golly, looks like we've got our man!" Doc yelled, waving the letter above his head. "You can bet your last nickel my old friend Adam Vestry wouldn't put his stamp of approval on a doctor who wasn't good enough for Eldridge." He stopped to read the signature. "Brent Palmer. Yessir, this may be it, folks. Get a wire off to him right away, Kitty."

"How old did you say he was?" The question came from Mr. Courtney, a retired farmer who had been under Doc's care for an arthritic condition over the past twelve years.

Doc scanned the letter. "Twenty-eight, I think he said. Yal, here it is. Twenty-eight."

"Awful young, wouldn't you say?" Bessie Steele, a thirtyish housewife who was expecting her fourth child, had arrived for a prenatal checkup as the morning mail was being delivered. "From what *I* heard, he's had no real experience at all!"

"Being a resident under Dr. Vestry?" Doc exploded. "On call in a big hospital for three years, just about every hour of the day . . . you don't call that *experience?*"

The woman looked uncomfortable under Doc's blustering attack, but she remained adamant, shaking her head dolefully. "After about ten years working on his own, I might trust a doctor, but. . . ."

"How many babies do you think I'd delivered 'on my own' before I brought you into the world, Bessie?" Doc's agitation threatened him with another collapse. "You want a doctor to start out in practice when he's sixty?"

The third party present, Mr. Courtney's wife, set her facial muscles in a grim, disapproving mask. "Twenty-eight. Why, my sons are older than that, and I wouldn't depend on a one of them to take out my gallbladder, like you say I'm going to have done. Bessie's right, Doc. We need somebody like you."

42

"Somebody who's past seventy and run out of steam!" Doc argued. "Well, if you've got all that much confidence in me, you'd better know I'm not going to turn you over to any doctor *I* don't look up to. We're damned lucky to find anybody at all, let alone a doctor with qualifications like these." Doc shook the letter at Mrs. Courtney for emphasis. "I'm not making judgments until I see what he can do, but I'm not going to let anybody malign him because he doesn't have a long gray beard, either. Dr. Palmer's going to have his chance, and I'd better not hear any more nonsense about his age. Some of your finest doctors. . . ."

"Oh, in *time* he may turn out pretty good," Mr. Courtney said in a pacifying tone. "Meanwhile, though, he'll be doin' his learning on us. Like, you might say, we're guinea pigs."

Bessie Steele and Mrs. Courtney exchanged knowing glances, obviously agreeing with the statement.

Doc added the letter to the clutter inside his rolltop desk, holding back his temper, but on the verge of another blowup. "You keep up that kind of talk! Next time you need a doctor in a hurry, you'll find yourself driving to West Fork."

Bessie Steele was quickly apologetic. "We know you'll do your best, Doc. We just thought . . . if there was somebody more like you. . . ."

Doc swung his massive frame away from the desk, shaking a thick finger at the expectant mother. "There's only one of me, Bessie, and I'm retiring. There's only one Dr. Palmer, and he's going to be here when your baby arrives, God willing. You ought to be grateful a young doctor's willing to come up here after what Kitty and I sent out in the way of a come-on. By golly. . . ." Doc turned to face Kitty. "By golly, when we sent out that ad did you think anybody at all was going to answer?"

Kitty made a wry face. "As a matter of fact, nobody did. And that journal's read by thousands of doctors all over the country."

"You didn't think any *established* doctor was going to drop his practice and come running to Eldridge, did you?" Doc was pacing the floor irritably. "We got exactly one reply! And that was through a friend who's been honored in so many journals he could paper a ballroom with the pages. Dr. Vestry's sending us a doctor, and *I* say we get ready to welcome him like manna from heaven."

Doc's tirade left his audience sheepish,

but, Kitty suspected, they were unmoved. It was regrettable, but it was understandable, too. For nearly half a century "doctor" was synonymous with "Doc Osgood." Anyone else, especially a twenty-eight-year-old stranger from Chicago, was going to be viewed as an upstart presumptuous enough to think he could replace an institution.

"Going to have a problem," Doc confided when he and Kitty were alone later. "These folks are so set in their ways it takes a dynamite blast to get them to change the way they part their hair, to say nothing about getting them to accept a new doctor." He checked his old-fashioned pocket watch, noted that it was twelve-fifteen, and started out the door for Aunt Emma's, where his unvaried Thursday luncheon would be waiting for him. "Can't get anything new into their lives without making a fuss. We'll have to use horse sense on 'em before Dr. Palmer gets here."

Kitty's fond smile followed Doc out the door. If Aunt Emma served anything but roast beef and baked potatoes today, Doc would think the world was coming to an end, and Kitty's attempts to modernize his bookkeeping system had struck him as a near sacrilege. He would have as much trouble adjusting to a new doctor being in

45

charge of these sacred premises as any of his patients. More. But Doc was arguing defensively because he had accepted something that the citizens of Eldridge would resist; he was no longer able to serve them, and his last obligation to these people was to prepare them for change.

By the first of July, Kitty had become a propaganda expert, helping Doc to "sell" his patients on the idea of a new doctor. But Kitty had not prepared herself for the shock of meeting Brent Palmer in person.

Young. It was the only word Kitty could think of as she escorted Dr. Palmer into Doc's office minutes after the flashy sports car pulled up in front of the hospital, disgorging the new arrival. He's *so young!*

Dr. Palmer had the fresh, youthful appearance of a college student. His handsome face and smartly tailored lightweight business suit were a glaring contrast with the turn-of-the-century decor of the waiting room, as though he had traveled backward in time from that fast-paced modern world outside, a world that Kitty had almost forgotten. His boyish face, crowned with a shock of wavy, chestnut-colored hair, was complemented by a slim, wiry build. Tall, in poised control of himself, the new doctor

46

made Kitty extremely conscious of herself. But apart from his breathtaking good looks, his first impression was one that worried Kitty. *They'll never give him a chance. Doc looks like everyone's idea of a doctor. They'll say he's just a kid and they won't trust him professionally.*

If Doc was equally startled, he disguised his reaction with a hearty, typically blunt welcome. Pumping Dr. Palmer's hand, he said, "Well, by golly, you didn't change your mind. Maybe you will after you've looked around. Sit down and let's chew the fat a bit, and then I'll have Kitty show you around. I'm still huffin' and puffin' from coming downstairs from my apartment."

Dr. Palmer had accepted the invitation to sit down, but Kitty noticed that he wore a somewhat bewildered expression. A first meeting with Doc was usually an overwhelming experience, and today Doc had come downstairs wearing, along with his baggy blue serge trousers, a red cotton plaid shirt with short sleeves that left his huge arms exposed, the somewhat seedy black string tie, and, because his feet had been bothering him lately, a pair of scuffy bedroom slippers that had seen better days. Hearing a nurse called by her first name had probably been another new departure for a doctor fresh out of a large hospital where formal protocol prevailed. He glanced questioningly toward Kitty, his smile tenuous. "Ah . . . I'd like to see the rest of the . . . building when Miss Simmons has the time."

"Oh, Kitty will make the time," Doc said in his most expansive tone. "We've got nobody coming in the next hour except Old Man Prevost with his gout, and he's likely not to show up if it clouds up anymore."

"But if he has an appointment. . . ."

Doc waved the young doctor's objection aside with his hand. "Makes no neverminds. We don't run this place by the clock. Folks can't get here, it's usually for a good reason. When they get around to it, it's 'cause they need us. Kitty and I just set our watches so's we know when to call for trays."

"Trays?" Brent Palmer's puzzled expression deepened.

"When we have patients hospitalized," Kitty explained. "We get their meals sent over from that little restaurant you can see from the window there."

"I see." Dr. Palmer may have seen the restaurant, but his vision of an efficiently operated hospital kitchen supervised by a university-educated nutritionist was abruptly shattered.

Doc patted his ample belly. "Emma gets the food here hotter'n the hinges o' hell, and you look at me and you can see she doesn't scrimp on the butter." He laughed at his own joke, then, in the interest of professionalism, added, "She can follow orders, too. Saline-free diet, ulcer diet, you name it, Aunt Emma can fix it . . . and, by golly, it doesn't taste like that slop they fed me when I was a resident. Best thing about this hospital, we don't feed our patients hospital food."

Dr. Palmer smiled. Apparently Doc had not thrown him. "I've checked in at the —" his smile broadened "— at the Ritz Hotel. I imagine I'll be having my own meals at this gourmet spot you talk about."

"Unless you want to drive clear to West Fork, you will," Doc said. "It's the only eatery in town." Doc turned and craned his head toward the window. "That your little jalopy out there?"

Kitty grinned. Doc had been away from the mainstream too long to recognize a customized foreign sports car that had probably cost more than all the Chevy trucks he had worn out in a lifetime of distant house calls.

Dr. Palmer was amused, too. "The jalopy was a gift from my parents. To celebrate the end of my residency."

Doc pulled out his heavy gold pocket watch and dangled it in the air, letting it swing like a pendulum. "Got this when they gave me my degree. My pa sold three sows to pay for it." He let the younger man admire the old-fashioned timepiece for a moment and then said, "You won't have much use for that little buggy out there, Doctor. Roads get rutted after a good rain here; you need a high wheelbase or you'd never get to your patients. It's okay, though. You use the ambulance. Besides, you might want to bring a patient to the hospital here. Can't cram 'em into that little crate of yours, can you, now?"

Dr. Palmer agreed that he couldn't, and shortly afterward Kitty left the two doctors alone, presumably to discuss the new arrangement.

More than two hours went by before Kitty began leading the newcomer on a tour of Doc's hospital, a tour that was interrupted by a mother whose four-year-old son had gotten washing bleach into his eye and a pair of teen-aged girls, one of whom had sprained her wrist practicing for Eldridge's Fourth of July baton-twirling contest. Since Doc had gone to Aunt Emma's for lunch, Kitty took care of both emergencies, managing them efficiently in spite of the watchful eye of Dr. Palmer.

They were leaving the small X-ray room, near the end of Brent Palmer's inspection, when he turned to Kitty and said, "The equipment is certainly adequate. I'd say some rearranging is in order, though."

In spite of the young doctor's personal attraction for her, Kitty found herself bristling defensively. "Oh, really?"

"Wouldn't you say so, Miss Simmons? Dr. Osgood's layout isn't — well, let me put it this way: If it weren't for the medical equipment I've seen, I'd think you've been showing me around somebody's home." Dr. Palmer raised his brows at a wicker rocking chair and ash tray stand in the hall. "Either that, or an antique shop. The place could certainly use some streamlining."

"If you mean that rocker, Dr. Palmer, that's Doc's tranquilizer for expectant fathers." Kitty was surprised by the resentment in her voice. She thumbed at a closed door near which the rocking chair was stationed. "That's our O.B. section. Labor and delivery. If the prospective papas couldn't sit out here, rocking and smoking, we'd have them under our feet." Pointedly, Kitty added, "I wouldn't make any changes until I've had a chance to see how we operate here, Doctor."

Kitty's critical attitude was reflected back from Dr. Palmer's eyes. They were calm, dark, observing eyes. As Kitty led the man who was to be — incredibly — her new superior into the waiting room, intending to acquaint him with Doc's original filing and billing system, Dr. Palmer nearly stumbled over the outstretched leg of a barefooted boy of about nine, one of three children who were gathered around the wobbly oak table. Regaining his balance, Dr. Palmer said, "I don't see an adult with these youngsters, but I presume they're patients. If you want me to. . . ."

"They're not patients *now*," Kitty said, waving back at a little girl who had grinned up at her from over a comic book. "School's out and they come here to read Doc's magazines."

Dr. Palmer was trying to absorb this last assault upon hospital efficiency, when another child, a twelve-year-old boy Kitty recognized as Tim Rafferty, burst into the room, breathless. Kitty hadn't noticed that during her tour with Dr. Palmer the rain that had been threatening for several days had begun in earnest; Tim's carrot-colored hair was plastered to his head, and his denim shirt and jeans were soaked.

"I ran . . . most of the way," the boy puffed. "Ma says Michael's real sick an' . . . can Doc get over to our house . . . right away."

"What's his trouble?" Kitty asked.

"He's got a . . . fever, he hurts in his stomach, an' he's tossin' up. Ma says if Doc could . . . hurry. She wants. . . ."

A clap of thunder drowned out the rest of Tim's sentence. "Doc's not up to going," Kitty decided. "He's liable to get stuck and it'll be too much for him. Dr. Palmer. . . ."

"I may as well get started now," the doctor cut in. "Where do I go?"

"Tim will show you the way. Let me get some dry clothes for him first." Kitty had crossed to the closet, where Doc kept a stock of forgotten and donated clothing for exactly this purpose, keeping up a steady stream of instructions as she searched for a shirt and jeans that would fit the boy. "The Raffertys live about eight miles from town . . . house overlooking Indian Rock Canyon. Tim's mother does Doc's cleaning here. I wondered why she didn't come in this morning. Look, we've had a rash of Asiatic flu going around, but this could be more serious. Doc's bag is on the desk in his office. Get that, and take the truck. If it stalls, Tim knows how to kick it over, don't you, Tim?"

"Yes, ma'am."

Dr. Palmer had hurried out of the room to get Doc's armamentarium. Kitty shoved the dry clothing at the Rafferty boy, told him to go into one of the examining rooms and change quickly before he added to his mother's problems with a cold, and then addressed the new doctor again as he hurried into the waiting room carrying Doc's battered black bag. "Take a minute to stop at Aunt Emma's. I'll phone her and she'll have a pot of chicken soup waiting as you pass by. Drop that off at . . . well, Tim will tell you where . . . on the way."

Brent Palmer looked incredulous. "I'm making an emergency call, Miss Simmons. I'm not running a catering service."

"It's for Hermit Joe," Kitty explained. "He's one of our patients, and he can't get out when it's raining. Doc *always* takes soup to him when he goes out toward the canyon. It won't take but a second."

Dr. Palmer was at the door, mumbling in disbelief. "Stop at Aunt Emma's. Deliver soup to somebody named Hermit Joe. . . ."

"Hurry it up, Tim!" Kitty shouted. She turned back to the doctor, her manner as brisk and direct as Doc's. "If you decide to bring Michael back here, let Tim come with you. The road may be a mess by then, and he knows how to handle the mud boards. They're under the cot, in back of the truck. *Timmy! Come on — you can finish changing on the way!*"

Tim raced out from the hall, carrying the dry jeans and his sopping denim shirt; he had completed only half of the clothes-changing operation. Kitty grabbed the "ambulance" keys from a drawer in the rolltop desk, pressed them into Dr. Palmer's hand, and hurried back to the desk to dial Aunt Emma's number. "I'll throw a canvas tarp over your car," she assured the new doctor. "Be careful about pulling up too close to the Raffertys' house . . . it's right on the edge of the canyon. Michael's not allergic to penicillin, if you need it. And please don't forget about Joe."

Dr. Palmer was probably too stunned to reply. Kitty completed her call, then watched from the window as Brent Palmer started up the truck, drove the short distance to the Ritz Hotel building through a torrential downpour, and took off again a few minutes later toward the unpaved road leading to Widow Rafferty's shack.

It was still pouring when Dr. Palmer returned, his elegant suit spattered with mud

55

and rain streaming across his face, as Kitty and Tim helped him to carry a cot bearing Michael Rafferty into the hospital.

"He's spiking a 105 fever," the doctor gasped. "We're going to have peritonitis to deal with if we don't open him up fast." The boy, two years Tim's junior, was eased onto a table in Doc's O.R. "Set up for an appendectomy, stat!"

Dr. Palmer had ripped off his wet jacket and shirt and was scrubbing. Kitty served as anaesthetist and scrub nurse, laying out the instrument tray and sponges, preparing and draping the field, taking time to scrub herself before helping Brent Palmer into a sterile gown and gloves. There was no time to go upstairs and to rouse Doc from his nap.

It seemed an eternity before Brent Palmer made the quick, clean incision, but no well-staffed operating room could have reached the infected organ faster. Serving now as an assistant, clamping bleeders and providing sponges, Kitty observed the young doctor's technique with a growing admiration. In Doc's prime, he could not have operated with more skill or a more certain knowledge.

When it was over, Kitty stationed herself at Michael Rafferty's bedside, nodding en-

56

couragement when Dr. Palmer came into the room, his expression apprehensive.

"He's coming out from under," Kitty whispered. She reported on the patient's temperature, pulse, blood pressure and respiration. "Couldn't hope for more, could we?"

The doctor shook his head. He looked blanched and Kitty noticed that his hands were unsteady as he recorded the observations. But there was a faint, lopsided smile on his face as he said, "You really play a lot of roles in this crazy . . . I *guess* I can call it a hospital. Where I come from, there'd be a recovery room nurse doing what you're doing now."

"The surgeon wouldn't have had to ram boards under the tires to get the ambulance out of a mire, either," Kitty said softly. She had an urge to compliment Dr. Palmer's gift for surgery, but she settled for peering at Michael's face. "Can't complain about his color, can we?"

Dr. Palmer made a shuddering motion. "I thought we were going to lose him before we got the truck out of that rut. My God, we were out in the middle of nowhere, knee deep in mud!"

"You've had your introduction, Doctor." Kitty smiled. "Not a typical case, but not exactly unusual, either. Mrs. Rafferty has seven kids. The law of averages says one or the other is going to have *something* wrong several times a year."

"That dilapidated shack, practically hanging on the edge of the cliff. . . ."

"The widow's very proud, Doctor. That shack is *hers,* and she can't afford anything better. Nobody here would insult her, offering free rent somewhere in town."

"Why, her medical insurance must run. . . ."

"She doesn't *have* medical insurance, Doctor. She has Doc." Kitty moved forward as their patient groaned, turned his head to one side, and resumed his drugged sleep. "You'll notice that the floors are immaculate here, Doctor. If you're wondering about your fee for this operation . . . the floors are going to go on being immaculate. Mrs. Rafferty's very conscientious about her bill."

Dr. Palmer appeared somewhat embarrassed. "I hope you didn't think I'm concerned about my fee."

"I'm sure you aren't," Kitty said. "You wouldn't have come here if you wanted to get rich." It was a compliment, and it deserved embellishment. "We can't say you've had your trial by fire. It's more like . . . an ordeal by mud. But you filled Doc's shoes today." Kitty looked up to find her eyes locked with those of Brent Palmer. "They're awfully big shoes, Doctor. Awfully big."

They looked directly at each other for a long moment, the rapport between them quickening Kitty's pulse. A deep sigh from Michael broke the thrilling impasse. Kitty got up to sponge the boy's face with a cool washcloth, and the doctor made a point of issuing his medication orders in a crisp, impersonal tone before he left the room.

He's going to stay, Kitty thought excitedly. He's going to be my neighbor at The Ritz, I'm going to work beside him every day, and I'll be able to respect him. He's terribly attractive, he's a good doctor, and he was able to come through in a rugged situation. Many another young doctor would have been on his way back to the city by now. But Brent Palmer was going to stay! And if the citizens of Eldridge were still dubious about his qualifications after today, they didn't deserve a doctor.

Four

Before the week was over, Doc had reached the same conclusion: If his patients failed to appreciate Dr. Palmer, crucifying him because of his youth or lack of "real experience," they weren't deserving of his services. Doc voiced a feeble complaint because he had not been called to at least observe the operation on Michael Rafferty, but, after watching the new doctor closely for a few days, he made it clear that he had no qualms about turning the hospital over to him.

Dr. Palmer's triumph was completed ten days after his arrival, when the Rafferty brood came to take Michael home. The days had been warm and sunny, and there was no problem in transporting the young patient home in the Chevy truck-cum-ambulance. For his contribution to the successful operation, Tim Rafferty was given a ride around town in the young doctor's sports car, and, afterward, since anyone who was kind to the impoverished but highly respected Rafferty family automatically earned the highest regard available in Eldridge, acceptance of Brent Palmer was assured.

Meanwhile, because Doc had full confidence in his successor, he began to spend most of his time in the cluttered study upstairs. "I've waited a long time to shift the burden," he told Kitty. "Now that I know my patients are going to get the best of care, I'm going to indulge myself, girl. Get my collections in order. Enjoy the few years I've got left."

Agreeing with Doc, Kitty was left with the responsibility of acquainting Brent Palmer with the *modus operandi* of Doc's hospital. There were individual eccentricities to be catered to. There were procedures that baffled the new doctor but had worked successfully; Kitty found herself being more zealous than Doc in maintaining the old ways and guarding against change. And because she knew the patients, knew exactly what Doc would do in any given circumstance, she managed the hospital, feeling justified and even helpful in issuing instructions to Dr. Palmer.

Her efforts were appreciated, she thought. One sweltering afternoon in the latter part of July, she was even convinced that Brent Palmer was grateful for her direction. With Mrs. Rafferty's help, she had just finished getting the closets in order after a delivery of sterile linens from West Fork. Walking to Doc's office (for in Kitty's mind it was still Doc's office) she met Brent Palmer returning from the waiting room. He had just walked an elderly patient to the door, and there was now the familiar bemused expression on his face.

"I'm glad you told me Mr. Neary has a thing about smoking. He beamed all over when I gave him strict orders to quit puffing two packs a day."

"Yes, he likes to be given doctor's orders to stop," Kitty said. "He claims it helps his self-control."

"Does it? I meant what I said. I could barely make out his ribs on that X-ray we took last week. That man's asking for trouble . . . if not cancer, a heart problem."

"He knows that. Mr. Neary wants to be *reminded.*" Kitty smiled. "Speaking of unbreakable habits, I was about to have coffee. I have a fresh pot going in the office."

"Can you pour a cup for a fellow addict?"

During the brief afternoon lull, Kitty poured several cups. It was the first time since his arrival that Dr. Palmer had taken time to relax; even when there were no patients to care for, he had been going through the files, familiarizing himself with case histories or writing out plans for improvement. Now he seemed to be noticing Kitty as a person for the first time.

"We won't go into my opinions of this whole operation," the doctor said. "We might get into an argument. Let me ask you why you're here. What are your plans? What kind of future do you see for yourself here?"

"I haven't had time to think too far into the future," Kitty replied. "I haven't even thought beyond the job I happen to be doing at the moment." She indicated the coffee cup in her hand. "There aren't many breaks like this, as you're finding out. There's always something to do."

"And you're happy here?"

Kitty hadn't thought about that either. "I feel useful. I don't feel my training's been wasted. Professionally, that's what we all hope for, isn't it? To know that we're needed — that we're doing a good job?"

"Apart from your work. . . ." Dr. Palmer had a way of probing beyond the surface as a physician; now he was applying the same meticulous analysis to Kitty's personal life. "Do you find the town interesting enough? Socially? You don't feel that you're stagnating here?"

"*You* might," Kitty acknowledged. "But remember that this is my home. I was born and raised in Eldridge. The people here are my friends. And. . . ." She thought for a moment, searching for words that would convey her sense of loyalty to Doc's hospital — his project and his dream. "I was born right here in this building. My mother worked here from the time she lost my father until she became ill herself. Somehow, in my mind, Doc's hospital is a sort of . . . shrine that has to be perpetuated. It's important to my people and it's got to go on. I just happen to fit in. It's where I belong, so . . . here I am."

"It can't stay the way you remember it from your childhood," Dr. Palmer said testily. "If a doctor doesn't move forward a mile a minute nowadays, he's not just standing still — he's moving backward. Just keeping up with a fraction of the new drugs, new equipment, new surgical techniques, is an overwhelming job. A hospital isn't a museum, Miss Simmons, or . . . somebody's favorite room in an old house. There's no place for sentiment or nostalgia."

Dr. Palmer's tone was not critical, but Kitty's innate defensiveness was stirred. "I happen to agree with Doc. Patients are people. Here they have names — they aren't just numbers. Why, I remember doctors and nurses in the big hospital where I worked referring to patients by their room numbers or their ailments. 'The hernia in 206' or 'the gastric resection in 329.' It's so . . . impersonal and cold, you'd think you were working in a plastics factory! Here we know everyone by name. We know the patient's family, his personal and financial problems. The kids aren't terrified about coming here when they're sick, because they're at home in our waiting room. Doc and I aren't just scary strangers in white. We. . . ."

Kitty stopped her harangue, aware that she was talking about the hospital as though Doc Osgood was still in charge. "I'm sorry. I didn't mean to exclude you, Dr. Palmer. But you *do* understand what I mean."

He nodded, stirring his coffee thoughtfully. "I know what you mean, and I'm in complete agreement about knowing the patient thoroughly. There's a lot of misdiagnosis occuring because doctors don't know the . . . family relationships, for example. Stresses that might produce tensions, tensions that might produce puzzling symptoms." Dr. Palmer hesitated. "I only wish you knew what *I'm* talking about."

Before Kitty's resentment could flare

again, the doctor added, "I realize that I'm too green here to get into a controversy. I was interested in hearing your views. I . . . hope you know I appreciate your efforts — helping me get acquainted. What I was interested in knowing about, were *your* plans."

"Oh?"

"I can't very well formulate my own without being sure that there's going to be adequate nursing services here. The shortage is acute in the cities. In a town like this, I don't imagine that good R.N.'s grow on trees."

"I'm afraid you're stuck with me," Kitty said. She had hoped that the conversation would lead to a date; hadn't the doctor expressed interest in her personal life? Disappointed, she assured him that she had no intentions of leaving her job, adding, "If I did, who would take my place? I'm the only nurse in town. And you'd get as many responses to an ad in the nursing journals as Doc got when he was looking for you. Zero. Eldridge isn't exactly the glamour capital of the world. And, as you say, a nurse can write her own ticket."

"That's why I've been asking questions," Dr. Palmer said. "Nurses have a way of getting bored with a dull place and leaving. Or getting married and quitting. Being neighbors at The Ritz, I couldn't help noticing that you don't go out a lot. Does that mean I shouldn't worry about the second risk and should concern myself with the first?"

His handsome face, still boyish in spite of the respect he had earned as a mature physician, wore such an earnest expression that Kitty forgot about resentments and disappointments and laughed. "I'm being wined and dined at the Danielsons' tonight, if that's any clue. Erma's decided it's high time I met the town's most eligible bachelor. You know how happily married women think. They can't stand the thought of anyone else being single."

Dr. Palmer got up from his chair behind the desk. "You mean there's someone in Eldridge you don't know?"

Kitty had hoped for a more encouraging, less casual response. To cover up her letdown feeling, she pretended indifference. "It seems I haven't met the new schoolmaster yet. Vernon Somebody."

"At least you're already on a first-name basis." The doctor was at the door, but he seemed reluctant to end their dialogue. "That seems to be the custom here. This morning I was told to call the bank president 'Harv.' Dr. Osgood gets furious if I

67

don't refer to him as 'Doc.' " He paused. "I suppose I ought to . . . start calling you Kitty."

Kitty rose to her feet. "I was wondering when you'd start. Everyone else does."

"And . . . at least when there aren't any patients around. . . ."

"I'll call you Brent." Kitty laughed again, holding her hand out for a handshake and saying, "How do you do," facetiously, as though this was their first meeting. The attempt at flippancy was lost in the warm contact of Brent's hand as it gripped Kitty's. She was suddenly ill at ease, her breath suspended, not sure whether she should be delighted or miserable. But, however she defined her emotions, there was no mistaking the fact that being this close to Brent Palmer had a profound effect upon her. It was as close to being in love, she decided later, as she had ever come. Closer. It was — confusingly, disturbingly — like the real thing.

Five

Kitty's dinner appointment that evening at the Danielson's began on a strange note. Dressing in her favorite summer frock, giving more than usual attention to her makeup and hairdo — wearing the long ash-blond hair in what she hoped was a sophisticated coronet of braids — she realized that all her efforts were not aimed at impressing a stranger named Vernon Olwyler. Being honest with herself, Kitty realized that she was hoping Brent would see her as she left the hotel.

Walking through the lobby, Kitty remembered that Brent made it a point never to leave the hospital unless she were present. He had taken to spending the nights in one of the hospital rooms and, encouraged by Doc, was thinking of moving out of the hotel. The Ritz, after all, offered no accommodations that weren't available in the big, brick building Doc called home. Besides, patients were accustomed to having a doctor in residence, and Doc enjoyed the company. Kitty proceeded toward the Danielson home, three blocks from the hotel, in a dejected mood — a mood not dispelled by Erma Danielson's obvious efforts to promote a romance.

There was no doubt that hours of effort had been invested in the dinner. The Danielsons' home, always comfortably homey, had been polished until it sparkled, and George Danielson's prize-winning roses decorated every occasional table that could hold a vase. Almost pathetically comic were the efforts of Kitty's hosts to pretend that this was just another dinner at home, the guests casually invited, with no ulterior motives involved. They were always charming and friendly people, of course, but tonight the Danielsons were working at it, demonstrating the advantages of married bliss, and the more they tried not to sound like matchmakers, the more they succeeded in doing so.

Vernon Olwyler was aware of their game, too. Fortunately he was not without a sense of humor, and, once, while the foursome was seated in the living room, with George Danielson expounding on the miseries he had endured years ago as a bachelor in a "lonely apartment," Kitty would have sworn that the new schoolmaster winked at her.

Vernon was probably in his early thirties, though his slightly receding blond hair and conservative suit may have added years to his age. He had an amiable face that was neither handsome nor unattractive. Taller and heavier than Brent, he gave the impression of a man who shunned extremes; he was average in appearance, neither dull nor stimulating as a conversationalist, neither rude nor stuffily polite in his manners. He was the sort of man you couldn't possibly dislike, but neither was there anything about him that ignited any romantic sparks.

At ten o'clock, when Vernon offered to walk Kitty home, their hosts lighted up as though they had executed a brilliant coup. At the door, they looked like a pair of lovesick honeymooners seeing their guests off.

"Wonderful people," Vernon said as he took Kitty's elbow, escorting her along the tree-lined sidewalk.

She could only agree, wondering if her tall companion's next comment would be about the weather.

It was. "Beautiful evening," he said. "It's not as warm and muggy as it's been."

Kitty dredged up some inane reply about the humidity being lower, now that the ground had dried up after the recent rains.

"It's a beautiful evening for walking,"

Vernon said. "I hope you don't mind? I live only a few doors from the Danielsons', so it wasn't worth taking my car out of the garage. But if you'd rather. . . ."

"No, no. This is just fine," Kitty assured him. "I like to walk."

"Do you? I've been doing a lot of hiking in the area. I love the outdoors. In fact, I was going to go back to Bismarck during the school vacation — visit my family and whatnot — but I've decided to stay here for the summer. I've organized a nature club for the seventh and eighth grade students, and we're having a great time collecting rocks and butterflies. . . ."

"You ought to get acquainted with Doc Osgood," Kitty told him. They discussed Doc's interests for a few minutes, Vernon enthusiastic about meeting a fellow nature lover, and after that there was an awkward silence.

Vernon finally broke into the quiet by asking, "Would you like to join us some morning? We take our lunches and hike out past Indian Rock Canyon. It's simply beautiful there . . . nice clear stream, big trees, and boulders. . . ."

"I'd love to," Kitty said. "Except that I don't have too much time off from the hospital. Dr. Palmer and I run the place without any help, you see, and . . . I really can't get away." Just mentioning Brent's name had given new life to the summer night.

(What would it be like to walk over to the hospital after she said good-night to her pleasant but unintriguing escort? Stop in — it wouldn't be hard to invent some pretext — find Brent alone and eager for company. Doc would be asleep by now, probably. They would talk. Brent would see her in this softly feminine blue print dress, wearing high heels instead of her sturdy white oxfords. Maybe, after they had talked for a while, Brent would. . . .)

". . . Arrange it sometime at your convenience," Vernon was saying.

Kitty snapped out of her wishful reverie, realizing that Vernon had been talking to her and that she hadn't heard most of what he had said. "Oh . . . at my convenience. Sure."

"Wonderful! You say when, and we'll be ready to go." Vernon's enthusiasm was almost childish. "Sunday afternoon? Or would you rather phone me? I'll tell you what, let's make it definite for Sunday, and if you can't make it, give me a ring. How does that suit you?"

"Fine." Kitty's thoughts wandered again as they turned the corner into Main Street, and the lighted windows of Doc's hospital could be seen beyond the illuminated sign on The Ritz Hotel. "That would be . . . just fine."

"Marvelous! You don't know how pleased I am. Perfect ending for a perfect evening." *He* hadn't been bored! He may have understood George and Erma Danielson's motivation in planning the dinner meeting, but he hadn't resented it one bit. On the contrary, as Vernon Olwyler saw Kitty into the dim lobby of her hotel, he said with complete sincerity, "I don't know when I've had a more wonderful evening. Meeting you, finding out that we have so much in common . . . it's been a real pleasure."

Kitty came up with a complimentary response, smiled, thanked Vernon for seeing her home, and was ready to head for the stairway when he said, again in an almost touchingly earnest tone, "I'm sure you'll enjoy the children. Very well-mannered and not as noisy as you might expect. I . . . know it wouldn't be proper to ask you out into the wilderness unless someone else was along. At least, not until you know me better."

Kitty concealed her astonishment; the man sounded as though he belonged to the same era as Doc's furniture. Heaven knew Doc, in his day, wouldn't have set up a date sounding like the more gentlemanly of the Rover boys!

"I'm sure I'd be perfectly safe if none of your students showed up," Kitty said. "But I'll enjoy having the kids around. They're not exactly strangers to me, you know."

"Of course. Of course, I forgot this is your home town. Well. . . ." Vernon grinned and stuck out his hand. "Goodnight, Kitty. Sunday at . . . say, around noon? I'll count on it unless you phone me. And . . . please try to get away. I'll be terribly disappointed if you can't."

He really would be disappointed, Kitty thought after she had reached her room. She had the disturbing impression that Erma Danielson's plan of intrigue had been at least one half successful.

Vernon Olwyler was erased from Kitty's mind seconds after they parted company in the lobby. Freshening her makeup before a dresser mirror in her room, Kitty felt the same nervous exultation that had preceded her first teen-age date. There was an element of adventure in going to the hospital at a time when there were no patients there who needed her, at an hour when Brent would probably welcome a visitor. Kitty inspected herself carefully, daubed a trace of her favorite scent behind her ears, and left The Ritz for the short walk to Doc's hospital and — hopefully — a new relationship with Brent Palmer.

Six

Kitty had entertained only a vague notion of what she expected from her impulsive visit. Whatever she had hoped for, however, was clearly not going to materialize. She knew it the moment she stepped into the waiting room.

Brent was standing next to the rolltop desk, and evidently he had been tearing it apart, drawer by drawer, because there were neat stacks of papers, medical journals, and file cards spread across the low oak table and over one of the wicker settees. He was obviously rearranging everything in the desk, because all the drawers had been emptied, and one sat on the floor near his feet.

Kitty's planned entrance — one that she had hoped would evoke an approving smile — collapsed, as Brent barely acknowledged her presence. He muttered, "Oh . . . hello," and went on with his project. One glance at his face revealed that he had been attacking the desk as though it were a personal enemy.

Kitty's heart sank; he hadn't even noticed her appearance. She felt suddenly awkward, wishing she had not obeyed the adolescent impulse. "I . . . thought I'd check in to see if everything was under control," she said. "There wasn't any message for me at the hotel desk, and you knew where to call me at the Danielsons', but I thought. . . ."

"As a matter of fact, I *did* leave a message at the hotel," Brent said curtly. He didn't turn around, crumbling a piece of paper in his hand and hurling it at the wastebasket. It missed, dropping to the floor. Brent gathered up several boxes of pharmaceutical samples that had been left by salesmen several weeks before and tossed them onto a pile of similar boxes on the settee.

Kitty suppressed her annoyance. It was like seeing Doc's private domain being violated, but she reminded herself that this was Brent's hospital now. Besides, she felt awkward in being here, and Brent seemed to be in an unusually surly mood. She had the impression that he had tackled this big physical job as an outlet for his energy and suppressed frustration. Kitty ignored the doctor's project. "I just came through the lobby. I wasn't given any message."

She was not prepared for Brent's sudden explosion. "That's just one more stupid aggravation I'm not going to tolerate any longer!" he shouted. He had spun around to face Kitty. "If I hadn't been able to handle the emergency alone . . . if there had been one more patient here, we'd have been in trouble."

"There's a new night clerk at the hotel," Kitty tried to explain. "He's an old man and maybe he didn't understand. . . ."

"They don't 'understand' because this place doesn't merit any more respect than . . . the local gas station! How do you expect people to regard this as a hospital when we let them use it as a library for their kids, a delivery service for oddballs who want to isolate themselves from civilization, a meeting place for every gossip in town! I had two women in this waiting room today working on a quilt! A *quilting bee,* for Pete's sake, while they were waiting for me to patch up this old character who'd dropped a root-beer keg on his toe. It was like a scene out of Alice in Wonderland!"

"That must have been Mr. Doheny and his two sisters," Kitty said. "Old Carl makes root beer in his basement, and. . . ."

"I don't want to know their life histories!" Brent exploded. He slammed a thick ledger down on the desk top. "I'm sick and tired of this casual, sloppy operation!"

"Sloppy?" Kitty's anger matched that of the doctor. "How can you say . . . ?"

"I'll say what I please!" Brent cried. "Partly because it's true, and partly because I'm in charge here. That's something else I'm going to establish. I'm the doctor in charge. I'm not going to be ordered around, told to do this and to do that because that's the way it's always been done. In every other hospital *I* know about the nurses don't give directions to doctors. They *take* them!"

Kitty felt her face burning. "I've only tried to be helpful. There's an awful lot you don't know about this town, Doctor. A lot you've got to learn about the patients."

"And the patients have a lot to learn about *me!*" Brent charged. "One thing is that I'm not going to put up with broken appointments without so much as the courtesy of a phone call. And then having people drop in whenever they're darned good and ready, expecting me to be at their beck and call." Brent rifled through the sheaf of papers in his hand furiously, then tossed them back on the desk in disgust. "I had a couple of hours here this afternoon that were straight out of an old Marx Brothers movie! The old goat with the smashed toe questioning everything I did, asking if I was *sure* Doc Osgood would approve what I was doing.

For two cents I'd have whomped him on his other foot, I was so irritated. Then, while he and those two quilty-brained spinsters who brought him in were still here, I had a foot laceration to patch up — another one of those grating episodes where the mother's careless enough to let her three-year-old daughter run around barefoot in an alley full of broken glass. But after she gets over her hysteria, she's not sure *I'm* intelligent enough to have done the right thing." Brent mimicked a shrill feminine voice: " *'I'd feel much better if Doc Osgood could have a look at it.'* "

"I'm . . . sorry about the blows to your ego," Kitty said. "We all have days like this. But the fact that people here are accustomed to Doc doesn't mean that everything here is wrong."

"It's not only wrong, it's medically unsound!" Brent had apparently had an exceptionally bad time since Kitty had taken time off late that afternoon. He was in a rage that demanded that everything be torn apart. "I put in that call for you — a call that I clearly identified as an emergency, by the way — because I wanted to be sure there was someone else here when a patient I suspect is either in diabetic coma or insulin shock gets here. A young woman . . . apparently on vacation with her husband and kids. Her husband called from some fishing lodge way out in the boondocks, wanting me to come out. I couldn't leave this place unattended, and, even if I hadn't gotten lost on the way — as I told the husband — he's better off getting her here where we can. . . ."

"Are they on their way?" Kitty asked.

"It's a two hour drive at least, the way I got it. It'll be a while before they get here. Meanwhile. . . ." Brent picked up the account book from the desk, plumped down into a wicker chair, and flipped it open. "Meanwhile, until I can make arrangements to have this alleged hospital adequately staffed, I'm starting with some of the more obvious messes that I intend to eliminate. For one thing, there aren't going to be any pharmaceuticals out here in the reach of anybody who happens to drop in. Especially not children!"

"The kids who come here wouldn't dream of touching anything on Doc's. . . ."

"It's *not* his desk!" Brent made the caustic point before Kitty could correct herself. "It's my *responsibility*, and if you knew anything about children, you wouldn't leave aspirin lying within their reach, let alone some of the drugs I've taken out of these drawers."

Kitty swallowed hard, knowing that he was right.

"I'll tell you something else that's going to change. The social atmosphere around here. I'm fed up with professional visits that turn into cozy little visits, and house calls that wind up with me being urged to stay for dinner . . . people getting their *feelings* hurt because I have other things to do."

Kitty opened her mouth to protest Brent's icy attitude. But before she could accuse him of being an antisocial snob who didn't understand Eldridge's warm, friendly people, Brent thumped the open record book with his fist.

"It's their looking at this hospital as a sort of community club that accounts for *this* mess. Pies, chickens . . . what do they expect us to do with produce, living in a hotel?"

"Well, Doc always. . . ."

"Always took the stuff to Aunt Emma's, I know. Well, from now on, if people can't pay a bill, they aren't going to be turned away, but they don't have to expect me to go carting groceries to a restaurant." Brent slammed the book shut. "And speaking of Aunt Emma's . . . from now on she's going to accept my money, like everyone else's. For breakfast, lunch, and dinner."

"She . . . lets me pay for my meals," Kitty

offered weakly. "But you've got to understand . . . she's never let Doc pay — not just because he gives her the hospital orders, but . . . well, he knocked himself out to save her son's life, back when Jeffie had meningitis, and ever since then it's been sort of a tradition with her. You're the doctor now, and Emma'd be terribly hurt if you insisted. . . ."

"I'm not merely going to insist, I'm going to make it stick. You can't run a hospital on this basis. That check for five hundred dollars that came in yesterday . . . you haven't explained what that's for. Am I suppose to believe . . . ?"

"It was from Nettie Craig, and that's all there is to tell."

"There's no record of her as a patient. I went out of my way to check."

"Mrs. Craig's never been sick a day in her life," Kitty said. She was finding it impossible to control her temper, listening to Brent's nit-picking criticism of everything that had always been naturally accepted during Doc's long regime. "She's a very rich widow. Every once in a while she contributes money to help us defray expenses for other people who can't afford their illnesses. It's her way of showing her thanks that she's never needed Doc's services. Big hospitals accept donated funds. Is there anything wrong with that?"

"This isn't a public institution," Brent countered. "It's a private practice, and it's going to be maintained like one. I mailed the check back this morning with a note to the effect that Mrs. Craig has no bill outstanding with this office."

"Oh, my stars!"

"Something wrong with that?"

"Nothing," Kitty hissed. "Except that Mrs. Craig is the recognized social leader in this town. She runs the women's club and the garden club . . . she knows everybody in Eldridge and owns half the mortgages besides."

"So?"

"So you couldn't have picked a more influential person to slap in the face, Doctor." Kitty was too distressed for first names; she placed a venomous stress on the word "doctor." "Incidentally, she's going on eighty, and she's told Doc that her will divides her money between a granddaughter and this hospital. Maybe some of the improvements you'd like to see could be made in the future."

Brent got up, dropped the account book on the desk, and grumbled, "The improvements I want aren't going to depend on

Mrs. Craig's convenient demise. Tomorrow morning I'll explain to you how I want the files and the accounts and the appointment book kept. There'll be no one allowed in this waiting room unless he or she is a patient or someone accompanying a patient."

"Doc's going to miss the children."

"Dr. Osgood, as he's been careful to point out to me repeatedly, is *retired*," Brent said. "He's a fine man and an excellent doctor, but he could have saved himself a lot of exhaustion if he hadn't made a neighborhood playground out of his offices. If his bookkeeping hadn't been so absurd, he might have been able to hire enough help to give round-the-clock nursing care to his patients, instead of depending on one nurse and an undependable hotel clerk."

Kitty's last shred of patience broke. "You've had a rough afternoon. All right — you're tired and irritable. That's too bad, because Doc had worse days, and after my mother died he had them without any help at all. He didn't complain and pick and go out of his way to make enemies. He took care of his patients as well as he could . . . and he didn't go around mewling because there's a nursing shortage. There's a shortage of doctors, too, in case you haven't heard. And the only thing that's kept *this*

85

nurse here is a friendly, unselfish atmosphere that you can't begin to appreciate — a wonderful feeling of community that you seem bent on destroying!"

Aggravatingly, because she detested revealing herself as a weak ninny, Kitty's anger brought tears to her eyes. Brent was looking at her with a calm smugness that only added to her misery. Certainly it was not the expression she had hoped for when she had looked at herself in the mirror, visualizing Brent's approval of the flattering blue print dress and all the other efforts she had expended to make herself attractive in his eyes. Kitty's disappointment demanded a release, and she knew, even as she gave vent to her frustration, that she would regret her culminating insult: "Maybe I was wrong. Maybe you can't adjust because you *aren't* big enough to fill Doc's shoes!"

Brent said nothing for a moment. The stillness in the room was almost unbearable. Then, still fixing Kitty with that infuriatingly cool expression, Brent said, "I didn't come here to enter a popularity contest, Miss Simmons. I'm a doctor charged with a responsibility, and I intend to discharge that responsibility *my* way, without any interference from you and without catering to any of the foibles Dr. Osgood tolerated. I took over a medical practice; I didn't inherit my predecessor's eccentricities."

"If you knew how much everyone in this town loves Doc. . . ."

"I share that high regard," Brent said in a freezing tone. "It isn't going to stop me from bringing this . . . so-called hospital kicking and screaming into the second half of the twentieth century."

Kitty searched for an argument, found none, and settled for reminding the doctor that there was one condition he couldn't change: He and his nurse were the only qualified people available to run the hospital. "If the hours are too long and sometimes it's too hectic, there's no one to blame because you can't *afford* to hire another R.N.," Kitty said. "If you quit. . . ."

"I don't intend to quit," Brent told her. "And I don't intend to be ordered around like a schoolboy just because you're more familiar with an out-dated way of doing things."

Kitty was not certain, at first, that she had heard Brent Palmer's final sentence correctly. It was a shocking revelation that she had time to mull over and despair over during the time before midnight when the patient they were waiting for was brought in. "I think I can solve the nursing problem, at least to a degree," Brent said. "My fiancée is an R.N. She'll be here shortly, and I expect to work out a more satisfactory schedule." He paused, apparently unaware of the emotional devastation he had just created. "The financial aspect won't be important. Christine's been doing part-time voluntary work anyway. She'll be interested in helping me develop a practice and won't expect to be paid."

Seven

It was strange, the way hostilities and resentments disappeared in the presence of a medical crisis. From the moment the terrified and exhausted young man helped Brent carry his barely conscious wife into Doc's hospital, the angry words that had passed between doctor and nurse were forgotten. No, not precisely forgotten: Kitty pushed her misery into a dim corner of her consciousness, to be revived later. Now she was part of a team once more, and a life hung in the balance.

The couple's children, two sleepy and bewildered little girls, were tucked into bed by their father, at Kitty's suggestion. Keeping the husband thus occupied kept him out of the way, a necessary move, because he had been almost incoherent with fear while Brent tried to extract a medical history from him. He was certain that the idyllic vacation he had planned with his family was going to end in tragedy, certain his wife was near death.

He was not far from the truth; the patient, as Brent had guessed from the phone conversation with her husband, was either in a coma or shock. Her complexion was a sickly blue-gray shade, and she was convulsing, threatening to choke to death as Brent made a hasty examination.

"I think we've got heart failure to deal with here — as though we needed a complication! Injectible digitalis," Brent ordered. He frowned as he continued his examination. "Her lungs are full of water, but she's bone dry otherwise."

Kitty had the digitalis ampules and syringe ready before the patient's arrival. The prescribed dose was injected in a matter of seconds. A blood-sugar reading, dangerously low, indicated insulin shock.

"Okay, let's get some sugar and water into her." As Kitty moved to set up an I.V., Brent shook his head. "No, she's too restless . . . we'd never find a vein, let alone keep a needle inside it. We'll slug down with paraldehyde and start an I.V. later. I'm going to get a Levin tube into her stomach first."

In the struggle that ensued, Kitty had no time to brood about the crushing emotional blow she had suffered. In spite of the patient's weakness, she struggled against the distressing procedure. Brent and Kitty were breathing heavily, shaken by a battle that should have been waged by muscular orderlies.

Every emergency procedure, it seemed, had priority. It was after one in the morning before the young woman was calmly at rest, a carefully controlled intravenous dose of sugar water restoring the delicate balance that had been upset. "You can't be too abrupt," Brent muttered. "She can leap from insulin shock to diabetic coma in nothing flat." He listened to the patient's heartbeat through his stethoscope. "Still fibrillating, but. . . ." Brent's facial gesture indicated that the digitalis had improved the patient's heart condition. More to himself than to Kitty, he said, "Her husband said she was under good insulin control when they took off on this fishing trip. We have this problem with diabetics . . . so afraid to go into coma, they overdo the insulin. This patient's supposed to be on sixty units daily. What'll you bet she doubled the dose this morning?"

Kitty made a disparaging motion with her head. "And going miles away from a medical service, with a heart condition! Doc and I had a case once, where. . . ."

She was cut off abruptly. "I'll watch her for the next hour. You might see how the husband's doing. Tell him we're not out of the woods yet, but we're getting control." Brent checked the needle in his patient's arm. "He might want some coffee. Rest for a while, and I'll call you if I need you."

Summarily dismissed, Kitty left the room to find the patient's husband pacing the waiting room, struggling against tears. After she had given the young man as much reassurance as she dared to give, fixed coffee for him, and checked on the sleeping children, she made an effort at sleep on Doc's old office couch.

Sleep eluded her. "My *fiancée*," Brent had said. He had never mentioned any romantic ties. But, then, he had told her next to nothing about his personal life. Why should it come as a shock to learn that he was engaged to be married? Handsome, personable (except when he was raving about the failings of Doc's hospital), evidently a member of an affluent family — was it so unusual to learn that some woman had staked her claim on Brent Palmer? (*Christine*. Her name was Christine. She was a nurse, and she would be coming here soon to help Brent effect the changes he was determined to make in Doc's hospital.)

Kitty wept over the changes, over the lost hopes, over the end of an era, over the ordeal of two young people who had planned a carefree vacation with their two little girls and ended up here, with the stricken wife and mother teetering between life and death. Disillusioned and weary, Kitty cried herself into a fitful sleep, waking up before dawn to relieve Brent, who had spent the night at his diabetic patient's bedside. By the time Doc came through the hospital on his way to Aunt Emma's for breakfast, the woman was conscious and apparently out of danger from insulin shock, though she would need several days of bed rest before she could return to the care of her own doctor.

"I just talked to him long-distance," Brent reported to Doc. "A Dr. Read. He wasn't even aware that his patient had gone out of town. He just about exploded when I told him she'd been out in an isolated area. He'd scheduled her for an EKG this week."

Doc made a clucking sound with his tongue, but offered no advice. "You've got everything under control," he told Brent after a brief discussion of the patient's treatment. "I would have done exactly what you did . . . probably not as fast." His confidence in the new doctor was so firm that he had done what Kitty would have sworn he could never do: divorced himself completely from the practice that had been his life.

Perhaps it was this attitude that made Doc unsympathetic when Kitty revealed her misery to him later that morning. During Doc's absence she had used the shower in his second-story living quarters, changing the now bedraggled dress for a fresh uniform. As Doc returned to the museum that was his study, he commented on Kitty's revived appearance, adding, "You looked like something the cat found on the stoop when I first saw you this morning. Guess you had a rough night." He settled himself in a mammoth plush upholstered chair that was just barely large enough to hold him. "I saw the patient's husband over at Emma's, getting some breakfast into his little girls. Nice young fella. Fell all over me when I told him his wife was resting easy. He's on his way over here by now, I expect."

"I'd better get downstairs," Kitty said. Except for the heavy sensation in her chest, she felt physically refreshed. "We're heavy with appointments this morning, and Dr. Palmer hasn't had any sleep."

"Yes, and you're going to have to watch that young woman like a hawk." Doc repeated the tongue-clucking sound. "Patient that doesn't have any better medical sense than that one . . . she's liable to decide to get up and go sight-seeing while she's here. I told her husband to take a room at the hotel and plan on staying a while. Poor devil. His eyes looked as bad as yours this morning." Doc lifted his brows, his expression inviting an explanation.

As briefly as possible, omitting the heart-breaking detail about Brent Palmer's fiancée, Kitty told Doc about her clash with the new doctor. "I don't know if I can stand the changes he wants to make," Kitty admitted. "Everything was going along so well, and now. . . ."

"Now it's Brent Palmer's practice," Doc said sternly. "And you aren't going to help matters one bit clinging to the past, young lady. It's *you* who's going to have to adjust. And, by golly, there's no room in a hospital for all this personal bickering."

"But he's going to wreck your practice if. . . ."

"*His* practice," Doc bellowed. "Get that straight in your mind, Kitty. It's Dr. Palmer's practice. I turned it over to him with no strings attached. All I expected was good medical service, and I don't think you'll question that."

"No, but I. . . ."

"No 'buts,' " Doc ordered. "You're a nurse working for a doctor. Maybe he's fed up with being pushed around, like you were his mother. . . ."

"I've only tried. . . ."

"You've only tried to help, but now he's had enough of that, and he wants to take charge. Can't blame him," Doc said. "Neither can you, if you stop and think about it. You come to me and tell me Brent's neglected a patient, and I'll go downstairs and raise all kinds of hell. But don't come around cryin' to me about petty, piddly, personal differences. Not when you've seen a doctor sitting up all night pullin' a patient through when she had the odds stacked against her. Nosiree, if Brent wants to paint the walls purple and set up a pool table on the porch, that's *his* business. *Yours* is to help him take care of his patients . . . with none of this damned quibbling. Understand?"

Kitty nodded, knowing that what Doc had said was true. Knowing it didn't ease her depression. At the door she said, "I just wish everything was the way it used to be."

Doc laughed, but there was nostalgia and even a trace of regret as he agreed, "Don't we all."

Kitty returned to her duties, wishing she had never complained to Doc. She had accomplished nothing except stirring up Doc's quick temper . . . and reminding him

96

that he was old. Furthermore, it hadn't even been an honest complaint on her part. All of Brent's proposed changes would have been tolerable. Even the addition of another nurse wouldn't have been upsetting; a second R.N. was actually *needed*. How could Doc have been expected to sympathize with the *real* cause for Kitty's sinking sensation? Brent Palmer planned to marry the new addition to the staff. And Kitty was in love with him. It was as simple as that. And as hopeless.

Eight

"It's been so wonderful these past two weeks," Vernon Olwyler said. "From the way you talked the first time we met, I couldn't decide whether you were really too busy to have time for me, or . . . whether that was just an excuse. Now I know you really couldn't spare the time then."

I shouldn't be able to spare it now, either, Kitty thought glumly. Since the diabetic had been released less than three weeks ago, the patient load at Doc's hospital had decreased steadily, until now there were whole mornings when Kitty had nothing at all to do except chat with Mrs. Rafferty while the latter cleaned the rooms.

Certainly there were no pleasant conversations with Brent Palmer. If he had noticed that his only patients were emergency cases, vacationers passing through Eldridge, or citizens with minor ailments, he made no comment about it. He occupied his free time streamlining and modernizing the hospital, asking for Kitty's help when it was needed in cooly formal terms, and suggesting afternoons and Sundays off for Kitty without being asked. Perhaps the long, unoccupied hours and the tense atmosphere were as disturbing to him as they were to Kitty, and when he said, "I think I can manage alone on Sunday," he was probably hoping to avoid another full day of strained silences.

This afternoon, Kitty had gone out on the second of Vernon's Sunday "nature hikes," happy to escape from her problems in a beautiful outdoor setting, delighted with Vernon's enthusiastic student friends and relaxed in Vernon's company. She had made a hasty judgment in thinking of the schoolteacher as dull. Perhaps he was not as exciting to her as Brent, but he was "old-shoe" comfortable to be around — thoughtful, pleasant, his outlook always positive. It was hard to visualize getting into an argument with Vernon. He enjoyed a warm camaraderie with his pupils without losing their respect, and Kitty found him a welcome relief after a day at the hospital — liked him well enough, in fact, to regard Vernon as a friend and confidant.

They had returned from their afternoon in the Indian Creek area early today, because

Vernon's neighbors, the Danielsons, had asked him to feed their pets while they vacationed for a week with relatives in Aberdeen. Kitty had accepted Vernon's invitation to "help me feed George and Erma's livestock," and, after the Danielsons' two dogs, three cats, canary, and parakeet had been fed, Vernon said, "If you're as starved as I am, Kitty, we've got our choice between Aunt Emma's counter and Erma's freezer. She said she was leaving all kinds of goodies that only needed to be heated. And she'd be, quote, 'crushed,' unquote, if we didn't help ourselves."

The "we" had slipped by unintentionally, Kitty suspected; apparently the druggist's wife had planned cozy little matchmaking suppers even in her absence.

"That's not really a choice, is it?" Kitty had said, grinning. "I haven't had a home-defrosted meal in ages."

It had been fun, making a selection from the Danielsons' amply stocked freezer, coming up with an unlikely but delicious menu that included sauerbraten, asparagus spears, and cheesecake, dining on their friends' old-fashioned screened summer porch and then tidying up the kitchen afterward. It had been more like playing house than visiting the Danielsons and being exposed to domestic tranquility, and it seemed perfectly natural to carry second cups of coffee out to the porch when the dishes had been put away.

"I know I keep repeating it," Vernon said as he settled himself next to Kitty on the glider. "But it's true. It's been another perfect day." He glanced at Kitty, the familiar look of naive bewilderment clouding his face. "You're smiling. Did I say something funny?"

"No, I was just wondering what you'd do if someone took that word away from you. 'Perfect.' You say it so often. And 'wonderful.' So many things are 'wonderful' to you."

The perplexed expression deepened. "You mean I sound like an immature Pollyanna."

"I didn't mean that at all," Kitty said fervently. "On the contrary. It's so refreshing to be around someone who isn't constantly finding fault. You enjoy life so much, it's . . . infectious."

"You really mean that? Oh, that's wonderful!" Vernon realized he had used the word again and laughed, Kitty joining him. After a few moments, he sounded more sober, as he said, "I imagine it must be rather grim at the hospital. What I mean is hospitals are always grim to me, but from what you've told me the place must be even deadlier with no patients coming in. When you phoned a while ago. . . ."

"I just checked to see if I was needed. I wasn't."

"I feel sorry for Dr. Palmer," Vernon said, meaning it. "How do you account for it? People driving all the way to West Fork to see a doctor when they have a perfectly good one right here in town. Just because he hasn't gone along with a lot of old, provincial customs?"

"Have you tried initiating any sweeping changes at your school?" Kitty asked.

"Well . . . no. Don't tell me the whole student body would withdraw en masse if I did."

"They might."

"I can't bring myself to . . . believe this is such a narrow-minded community," Vernon said between sips of coffee. "I've met so many wonderful people here. . . ."

"Doc Osgood's wonderful, too. But he hasn't changed his suit style since he got out of med school."

"Yes, but you said he was willing to let Dr. Palmer run the show his way."

Kitty sighed. "Let's just say Doc's a little more just than some of the people in town.

Besides, he's removed himself from the picture. Patients can't escape being involved."

"And they're boycotting the hospital for all those silly reasons you told me about? Cutting out the juvenile reading room and . . . trying to run the place on a halfway businesslike basis?" Vernon shook his head back and forth slowly. "It's beyond belief. Misguided loyalty, I suppose. And, then, the whole world's going through so many radical changes, I imagine people — especially old, established people — want to hang onto every last scrap of security. Insofar as the familiar represents security, that is. In this case — wasting time going to another town to see a doctor, is not only absurd, it could be downright dangerous."

Kitty listened to the impartial view, admiring Vernon's fairness and logic, wishing that she had not contributed to Brent's frustration and his resulting demand for "reforms." Brent's changes seemed insignificant now; some, although she had not admitted it to the new doctor, had substantially improved the efficiency of Doc's hospital, freeing Brent and herself to give closer attention to medical problems. Yet there were so few appointments on the calendar — the new, systematically kept calendar! — that the improvements seemed futile.

"Does Dr. Osgood know what's happening?" Vernon asked.

"He can't help knowing," Kitty replied. "He's been trying to ignore the truth. Keeping his promise about not interfering. But he's probably miserable. And he's been so quiet, I'm dreading an explosion."

"Not aimed at Dr. Palmer, I hope?"

"Heavens, no. At anybody and everybody he meets on Main Street. Widow Craig, first of all. I'm only guessing, but I have an idea she hasn't helped the situation."

Vernon was genuinely concerned, even though he only knew most of the people mentioned by name. "Couldn't you talk to this . . . Mrs. Craig?"

"You still don't know this town, Vernon. If you did, you wouldn't expect me to tackle an eighty-year-old martinet . . . who practically runs Eldridge. Even Erma Danielson wouldn't take *her* on. Erma's no lightweight, and she likes Dr. Palmer."

"Maybe she doesn't know. . . ."

"She knows what's going on," Kitty said. "Why do you think the Danielsons took their first vacation in ten years? Because Dr. Palmer hasn't written enough prescriptions in the past few weeks to merit keeping their pharmacy open. People are getting prescriptions filled in West Fork next door to the hospital there, where it's handy. Poor Doc. If he knew that. . . ."

Tears had sprung to Kitty's eyes, and she was barely conscious of the comforting arm that had fallen over her shoulders. "Cheer up," Vernon urged. "It's bound to get straightened away. Come on, now, Kitty. Let's not spoil a marvelous day like this with tears."

Kitty felt her chin being tilted upward. Then, as she tried to erase the disturbing thoughts from her mind, knowing it was unfair to burden Vernon with problems that didn't concern him, she was surprised by a gentle kiss on her forehead.

"I don't like to see you unhappy," he said softly. "I've grown very fond of you, Kitty. I wish . . . I keep hoping you'll be happy enough with me so that nobody else matters."

Vernon's sincerity was always touching. He was one of the rare, totally unselfish people who were regarded as naive, even anachronistic, in sophisticated circles. How peaceful and uncomplicated life would be with this man who tried to see everyone else's viewpoint, who was as sympathetic with the trials of a doctor he did not know as he was with the sometimes incomprehensible people whose children he had chosen to teach!

For a fleeting moment, Kitty was tempted to return the shy kiss, to let Vernon take her into his arms and offer the affection and understanding for which she hungered. But then, knowing that hers was only a temporary mood, she decided that Vernon's honesty didn't deserve to be used. More important, it would be a shoddy trick to offer him encouragement. "You're a . . . real friend," she said lamely. (What else? What more could she say to someone who was looking at her with that imploring expression in his eyes, waiting for her to extend the hope that she shared his sentiments?)

Vernon was extremely perceptive, and Kitty's pause had lasted too long. "That's it, then," he said. "You couldn't ever see me as anything more than a friend."

"Oh, I like you immensely," Kitty assured him. "You know that. I relax completely when we're together, and I've had more fun. . . ."

"We aren't talking about the same thing." Vernon sounded morose, but not self-pitying. He lifted his arm from its contact with Kitty, hiding his nervousness by pretending interest in what was left of the coffee in his cup. After an uncomfortable silence, he said, "I'm afraid I've been assuming too much. Thinking like Erma

Danielson. Everything all cut-and-dried. You're single, I'm single, we get along beautifully — all that's needed is some time and a perfect setting." He released a short, disparaging laugh. "It isn't as simple as all that, is it, Kitty?" Strangely blunt for someone whose approach was always cautious, he said, "Are you in love with someone else?"

Kitty lowered her head. "I don't know. I. . . ."

"Dr. Palmer?"

Kitty hesitated, then nodded. "It's all so muddled. And so pointless. Honestly, Vernon, I wish. . . ."

"Don't apologize for something you can't help. I may be simple, but I'm not an adolescent." Vernon got up from the glider, crossing to the screen door and looking out over the Danielsons' rose garden. "I hope you'll believe me, Kitty, when I say I wish you the best of luck. Palmer's a fortunate man. And he must be a wonderful person."

"He's an engaged-to-be-married man!" Kitty said sharply.

Her tone must have startled Vernon. He spun around, facing Kitty with a look that was half-incredulous, half-compassionate. After a while he said. "I'm sorry. I'm truly sorry. Are you positive? If there's ever anything I can do. . . ."

There was nothing he could do, but Kitty thanked Vernon Olwyler for his offer. They talked about the irony of unrequited love for a few minutes, keeping the conversation on a philosophical rather than a personal level, and then, probably because he realized there was no more to be said, Vernon made a deceivingly sprightly suggestion that "even wonderful days have to end sometime" and, face it, they were both tired from the long afternoon hike.

Between the Danielsons' home and The Ritz, they discussed inanities, Kitty wishing that there was some way that she could express her regrets without adding embarrassment to Vernon's disappointment. There was no way to do so, and they parted as though nothing had transpired between them, as though their next time together would, again, be "perfect." That it would never be the same again went without saying.

Nine

There was an oppressive atmosphere inside Doc's hospital now. Brent Palmer's realization that he was failing, coupled with an obstinate determination to stick it out and succeed, had changed him from a self-assured young physician to a picayunish tyrant. Perhaps he was castigating himself when he expressed annoyance over unimportant little details, but Kitty bore the brunt of his complaints, feeling alternately angry with him and sorry for him.

During the long lulls between patients, Kitty busied herself with tasks that were a far cry from the fulfillment she had enjoyed while working for Doc. There were times when Brent isolated himself in his office, and Kitty knew that behind the closed doors he had dropped his pose of being the busy M.D. engrossed in modernizing an outdated institution. It was more than likely that he sat at his desk brooding, wishing he had never set foot in Eldridge, yet too proud to give up the project as a failure.

Several times, after hearing Brent talking to Doc and feigning complete confidence in the future, Kitty was nearly overcome by a yearning to comfort both doctors. Yet Doc and his successor had little left now except this pseudo-bold masculine front; condolences from Kitty would only have depressed Doc and irritated Brent.

Besides, Doc was making a studied effort to separate himself from the hospital completely. "Hell's bells, I put in my years down here," he told Kitty one morning, apropos of nothing at all. "I earned my rest, girl, and now I'm enjoying it. Got a young crony to enjoy it with, too. That young fella you sent over to see my collections, Vern Olwyler, by golly, there's a lad that knows his natural history! We were up past midnight last night, reclassifying my butterflies and mounting a display."

Vernon's first visit to Doc's quarters had firmly established him as the old man's friend, though Kitty suspected that curiosity about Brent Palmer and herself had also drawn the schoolmaster to the premises. It didn't matter. Doc enjoyed the stimulation of another man who shared his various interests, and there were times when she, too, welcomed a few words of conversa-

110

tion that weren't laced with gloom. Seeing Vernon pass through the hospital corridor on his way upstairs the day before had been better than seeing no one at all.

The empty rooms — occupied only occasionally by a vacationer with a case of poison ivy or one of the few local residents who remained loyal to Doc's hospital, if not its new director — seemed charged with the electricity that precedes a storm. It's like a pressure chamber, Kitty thought. It can go on this way for just so long, and then something's got to happen.

Kitty was having her lunch at Aunt Emma's when the storm broke. Waddling up to the counter after answering the wall phone in her kitchen, Emma addressed Kitty in terse syllables. "Better get over to the hospital, dear. Dr. Palmer says it's an emergency."

Kitty left her barely touched plate and raced out of the café without a word. Running toward the red brick building, she saw a familiar-looking truck parked in the driveway. Running, she drew nearer and made out the yellow-lettered sign on the truck's door: PINE TRAIL STABLES. Someone at the horse ranch just outside Eldridge had probably been injured. Kitty covered the remaining distance like a sprint champion, gasping for breath as she hurried through the hospital waiting room.

There were two young men standing near the corridor to the emergency room; Kitty recognized them as employees of the riding stable. Either of them would have qualified as patients: their faces, in spite of the deeply tanned complexions, looked bloodless.

"What happened?" Kitty asked, as she made her way past them.

"This girl rented a horse . . . reined it to a fast halt and got thrown," one of the men reported.

The other's words followed Kitty as she pushed open the emergency room door: "God, that stallion rolled clean over her. Looks to me like she's dead!"

One glance at Brent's face corroborated the layman's guess. Brent was working frantically over the still form of a girl whose slender figure indicated that she was in her early teens, but whose face and arms, a deep blue-black in color, defied description. A thin stream of blood trickled from the side of her mouth and from the ear that was visible through a tangled mass of red-gold hair.

Kitty jumped at Brent's orders, though it was plain to anyone who had ever worked in an emergency room that the doctor's orders were futile. Brent knew it, too. The patient had been subjected to a crushing weight, suffering internal injuries to every vital organ. It was too late for exploratory surgery, too late for any medical miracle.

"I don't get a pulse, Doctor," Kitty said as she confirmed Brent's suspicion. There was no heart action at all, no discernible respiration in spite of the oxygen mask Brent had applied.

Brent made a desperate attempt at revival, refusing to give up even in the face of the obvious. He had taken every emergency measure possible, and minutes had dragged by before he looked up at Kitty over the lifeless body and whispered, "She's gone. She's out of our hands now, Kitty."

Disconsolate, Brent verified his statement, leaning over the motionless form and going through the prescribed rituals. Kitty detected tears in his eyes and his lips moved soundlessly, as if in prayer. Another eternity passed before he straightened up and muttered, "She was God's youngster when they brought her in. I just couldn't . . . let myself accept it."

Kitty moved slowly, removing the mask, cutting off the now useless oxygen supply, and finally covering the girl with a sheet. She would probably never forget that tousled hair, still glistening like sunlight as Kitty drew the cover over it. The girl had worn a jaunty yellow scarf to brighten her beige riding clothes. Somewhere, somebody was waiting for her to come home.

Brent was at the far end of the room, facing the wall. "There . . . there wasn't anything you could do," Kitty murmured. The words bounced back at her, echoing through the nearly empty room, hollow and meaningless. She waited for a few more seconds and then said, "I'd better tell the people outside. We'll have to notify her family."

She saw Brent's slow nod, whispered, "I'm so sorry, Doctor," and slipped out of the room.

It wasn't necessary to give her report to the young men waiting outside the door; they glanced at Kitty's face and knew that their wild race to Doc's hospital had been futile.

Before Kitty could ask how the girl's family could be notified, the taller of the young men said quietly, "It's going to be rough, breaking this to the old lady. For her, I guess the sun rose and set with that kid. Melissa was her granddaughter."

His companion was apparently unacquainted with the girl's identity. "Who's that, Jerry? What old lady?"

"Mrs. Craig. Boy, you oughta know *her*. She owns the mortgage on your pa's ranch. You'll probably have to get ole Nettie Craig's permission before you shoot that crazy stallion."

Kitty released a long sigh and crossed the waiting room toward the rolltop desk. No one else was going to make the phone call to the eighty-year-old woman who had worshipped a pretty youngster with golden-red hair. It was a duty that couldn't be avoided, but no one could have blamed Kitty for hands that trembled as she looked up Nettie Craig's number and began to dial.

Ten

A pall of gloom settled over Doc's hospital after the accidental death of Melissa Craig. The cloud that fell over Eldridge was less silent. In spite of the testimony of the young men who had rushed the girl to the nearest medical facility, the town buzzed with controversy. Impassioned voices were hushed as Kitty stepped into Aunt Emma's café, into the bank or the drugstore, and a thick silence would follow. But the theme of those abruptly terminated discussions was inescapable; if Nettie Craig's granddaughter had been brought to Doc Osgood, he would have saved her life. The new doctor, "barely old enough to shave," "high-handed, with all his fancy ideas" hadn't known what to do. An experienced, competent doctor would have kept the lovely young visitor alive. Such a beautiful *young* girl, full of laughter, rich, everything to live for. . . .

More than once, Kitty found herself starting to lash out at the injustice of the vile gossip campaign, but there were no accusers to face. There were only the abruptly ended dialogues when she stepped in on impromptu gatherings . . . then silence and sheepish or righteous expressions.

Seeing Brent's agony (what doctor ever forgot the first patient who had died in his care?), Kitty visualized the effect similar scenes were having upon him. And there was no doubt that he was aware of the ugly whispering campaign; he spent more time in Doc's old office. He said only what it was necessary to say — and that, in a solemn, lifeless undertone. Loving him meant sharing his misery, yet Kitty's attempts to cheer him up were coolly avoided. How could she expect to convince Brent that he had her confidence and respect? Wasn't she the first person in Eldridge who had accused Brent Palmer of being too small to fill Doc Osgood's shoes? The memory of those bitter words burned Kitty's conscience. If she remembered them, how could she hope that Brent had forgotten?

Burning with frustration, dreading the endless days at the hospital now that it was all but deserted, Kitty stayed on the job only because of Doc Osgood. At least she told herself that it was only concern for Doc that kept her in Eldridge; her unspoken devotion to Brent Palmer was a stronger magnet. Brent had said nothing more about the arrival of his fiancée. Was it only because a second nurse was no longer needed? Or was there still hope that if Kitty proved her loyalty to him he would someday return her love? If she fled from this dismal situation she would never know.

On a muggy afternoon in August, Kitty was asked to accompany Doc to the Eldridge bank. It was a mission she deplored: Doc was transferring funds from his small savings account to help defray hospital expenses and to cover Kitty's salary.

While Doc transacted his business at the teller's window, Kitty chatted with George Danielson, one of the few old-timers in Eldridge whose confidence in the hospital was unshaken. Discreetly, George made no mention of the problem, though Doc's loud voice had revealed his purpose in visiting the bank. Talking purposefully about the mildew that was attacking his roses, the pharmacist stopped suddenly and muttered, "Oh, no! Look."

Kitty followed his gaze through the plate-glass window to see an ancient but immaculately polished black Lincoln pulling into one of the parking spaces at the curb. As she watched, a uniformed chauffeur leaped out to open the back door, helping a black-clad old woman out of the car. White-haired, her face a frozen gray mask, Nettie Craig emerged, waving her driver aside impatiently and covering the steps to the bank briskly, with the help of a cane.

George Danielson leaned forward to whisper, "Has Doc seen her since . . . ?"

Kitty shrugged her answer: "I don't know." Doc and Mrs. Craig had been old friends, and he had certainly sent his condolences, but Melissa's funeral had been held in Minneapolis, where she had attended school and where her parents, now deceased, had lived. Nettie Craig had gone to attend the services and, since her return to Eldridge, had remained secluded in her rambling old mansion on Crestview Road. The sight of the old woman now, gaunt and rigid in her bearing, sent an inexplicable shudder through Kitty.

Mrs. Craig tapped her way past George Danielson and Kitty without noticing them. Her colorless eyes seemed to look past everything and everyone, as though she were looking toward a bleak landscape beyond normal vision. In spite of the woman's age, she had always been hyperactive, charged with a bristling energy. Now, although she

119

still moved with her familiar birdlike quickness, she resembled a living corpse.

As Mrs. Craig walked toward the counter, Doc completed his transaction and turned to leave. The old woman's path was blocked by Doc's massive body. Towering over Mrs. Craig, standing before her like an impassable wall, Doc's recognition was immediate and sorrowful. "Nettie," he said. He had never spoken more quietly before. "I've been trying to call you. The housekeeper tells me. . . ."

"Mrs. Parrish has her orders," Mrs. Craig said. Her tone was brittle and chilling. "I am not to be disturbed."

"I thought you might want to see old friends." Doc's face creased in a tender halfsmile. "Nobody has to tell me what a loss you've suffered, Nettie. You've always been a strong woman, but there are times when we need our old. . . ."

"Benjamin Osgood, you are no friend of mine!" Mrs. Craig's words crackled through the wood-paneled bank lobby. The few customers and clerks stared toward the two old people, tense and motionless.

"Nettie, you know that. . . ."

Doc's plea was cut off with a savage, broken cry from Nettie Craig. "If you were my friend you would have been there when

Melissa was brought in. You wouldn't have left her to that . . . that. . . ." The old woman shook her head, unable to express her bitterness. Then, in an imperious tone, she said, "Let me pass, please. I have business here."

Doc's face had turned scarlet, but he didn't budge. "Nettie, no one's more miserable over what happened than Brent Palmer. Don't you understand — there wasn't anything he could do. Melissa was gone when. . . ."

"Don't mention that quack's name in my presence!" Mrs. Craig shrilled. "And don't use Melissa's name in the same breath!"

"*I* couldn't have saved her!" Doc cried. His bulky frame had started to tremble, and Kitty shot a concerned glance at George Danielson. "We're only doctors. We aren't God. I've got all the sympathy in the world for you, Nettie. I'd give my life if I could bring that child back to you. But I'm not going to let you destroy a fine young doctor because he couldn't work a miracle. I know what this has done to you. I'm one of your oldest friends . . . do you think I don't know?"

"You *can't* know," the old woman croaked. "If you had. . . ."

"*If I had been there, Melissa would have died*

121

and you'd have blamed me!" Doc thundered. He was shaking dangerously now, the veins standing out at his temples, threatening to burst. "By God, Nettie, I've seen enough sickness and death in my life to bow my head before another person's grief. But I can't respect a mourning that's vindictive and vile. You aren't going to bring Melissa back by ruining a young man who tried . . . whose whole life is dedicated to. . . ."

"Have the decency to let me mourn in peace," Mrs. Craig hissed. Her wrinkled face remained immobile, and Kitty noticed that her eyes looked beyond Doc, as though he had ceased to exist.

Doc stood his ground for a moment. Then, his big arms dropping to his side helplessly, he stepped to the side, allowing the black-clad old woman to pass. He was breathing heavily as he walked over to where Kitty stood. It must have taken all of his strength to nod cordially at his pharmacist friend and say, "How you doin', George?"

George was too shaken by the incident to show equal control. He reached out his hand to give Doc a comforting pat on the arm.

"We'd better get you back to your room," Kitty said softly. She locked her arm through Doc's, guiding him out of the building and into the sultry heat of Main Street. His aguelike trembling alarmed her, and Kitty walked slowly, her fingers pressing Doc's forearm in a firm, reassuring grip. Untypically, Doc walked slowly, too, allowing himself to be led. It was best to say nothing, Kitty thought. There were no words with which to console Doc now.

A dusty new Cadillac was parked in the hospital driveway. Because the tense silence had become unbearable, Kitty pointed it out as they approached the red brick building. She made an attempt to sound sprightly as she said, "You see, Doc? We still have patients. New ones who can afford the best."

The quip failed miserably, sounding ironic and depressing to Kitty even as she made it. She turned to look at Doc's face and then averted her gaze just as swiftly. Huge tears were rolling down his cheeks. Kitty held back her own, her love for Doc too intense at this moment to let him know that she had seen him crying.

Eleven

Fortunately, Kitty was able to get Doc up to his living quarters without encountering the owner of the Cadillac. On closer observation, its Illinois license plates had told Kitty that her guess was wrong: The car didn't belong to a new patient. It had probably been driven from Chicago by Brent Palmer's fiancée. The door to Brent's office was closed, as Kitty walked by with Doc. She thought she heard not one, but two feminine voices from behind the door. It didn't matter. Her morale was already too low to suffer further damage.

Doc had been spared the torture of having to be pleasant through a round of introductions. There was a second blessing in the form of Vernon Olwyler, who smiled up from his place in Doc's study. "Hi, Doc . . . Kitty. I feel like a burglar, but Dr. Palmer said it would be all right to wait for you up here." Vernon gestured at a disarray of colorful mineral specimens before him. "I brought some of my duplicates over. If you have time, maybe we can do a little swapping." Typically, Vernon pretended that he hadn't seen Doc blotting his face with a huge red kerchief. "Just don't think you're going to get this fantastic amethyst crystal for some of your old mica slabs."

As Doc edged forward for a better look at the violet specimen Vernon held out to him, Kitty breathed a prayer of thanks. Saint Vernon! He wouldn't *allow* anyone to be miserable in his presence.

Doc would be a long time getting over his traumatic experience at the bank, but at least it wasn't necessary to patronize him by asking if there was something that could be done for him. He had made a determined effort to square his shoulders, and as Kitty started to leave the room his voice was almost normal! "I've got a geode that's worth ten of these, Vern. Don't try any of your city slicker salesmanship on me."

Vernon's eyes traced Kitty's exit from the room, as they always did. This time, replacing the usual worshipful expression, he looked faintly bewildered as Kitty formed a soundless "thank you."

Brent was no longer in his office; the door was wide open, and the room was deserted. A painful "ow!" directed Kitty to one of the examining rooms, where Rosalie, the next-to-the-youngest carrot-top in Mrs. Rafferty's brood, sat on the table while the doctor swabbed her left foot with an antiseptic solution.

"Why didn't you call me, Doctor?" Kitty asked. "I was just upstairs with Doc."

Brent turned to acknowledge the offer with a humorless smile. "Nothing I can't manage myself. Rosalie was playing in the back yard and stepped on a burr. We'll slap a bandage on it, and we're all set, right, Rosie?"

"It doesn't even hurt any more," the little girl announced.

Brent had done so little doctoring in the past few weeks that it seemed unfair to step in and complete the minor task. Kitty exchanged a few pleasantries with the six-year-old and wandered toward the waiting room, hoping to find something constructive to do. A cloud of smoke and an incredulous, mature female voice greeted her as she entered the room:

"I'm not even certain that a rummage shop will want this trash, dear. Brent has such excellent taste, I wonder he hasn't had it dragged out and burned."

Kitty saw the speaker first: a well-proportioned, statuesque woman in her fifties, beautifully tanned, her sun-bronzed face contrasting smartly with shortly clipped hair that had been tinted a subtle champagne-blond shade. She wore a simple but chic dress of lime-green linen accented with frosty white accessories. Even on this wiltingly humid day she looked poised and cool.

Kitty's glance shifted to a younger, thinner counterpart of the matron; they were obviously mother and daughter, although the girl's hair was black and worn in a casual shoulder-length style. Their distinctive green eyes were identical, however, as were their classic features, country-club tans, and rather elongated faces. Dressed in dark green capris, a white tailored blouse, and unique leather sandals, the daughter was a study in conservative understatement. She sat stiffly on the edge of one of the wicker chairs, as though she disdained closer contact with anything so shabby.

Uncomfortable in their presence, Kitty nevertheless introduced herself as "Miss Simmons, Dr. Palmer's nurse."

The brunette's face was hardly disturbed by a polite smile. "I'm Christine Westbrook. This is my mother, Mrs. Westbrook."

Kitty nodded, said, "How do you do?" and hoped that her glance at the engagement ring on Christine's left hand had gone unnoticed. She forced herself to ask if the visitors had had a pleasant trip, wishing that she felt less resentful; after all these strangers had committed no crime.

"It was just barely tolerable," Mrs. Westbrook replied. She ground her cigarette out in the fern planter and examined Kitty with a patronizing smile. "Have you worked here long, Miss Simmons? It seems such a dull place for a young woman to choose."

"I was born and raised in Eldridge," Kitty told her. She crossed to the desk and feigned interest in a stack of circulars from pharmaceutical houses.

Mrs. Westbrook said, "Oh, really? How interesting," in a tone just short of incredulous.

"I suppose you were here, then, before Dr. Palmer?" Christine asked. Her long fingers gestured dismissingly at the room and its furnishings, indicating that Kitty belonged to an era that had passed. "You worked for. . . ."

"Doc Osgood," Kitty filled in.

There was a frigid pause, then Mrs. Westbrook said, "It's such a contrast with my husband's practice. I imagine you've gotten accustomed to the . . . slow pace." She addressed the next sentence to Christine. "Though I can't imagine Brent enjoying this lack of activity. I don't think we've seen but one patient since we arrived."

Kitty started to tell the woman that not long ago Doc had hardly been able to keep up with his practice, that he had exhausted himself taking care of too many patients. She checked herself and said, "It varies, Mrs. Westbrook. Just a few weeks ago, Dr. Palmer felt we needed another nurse."

"Yes, he wrote to Christine about that," Mrs. Westbrook said. "My daughter's an R.N., you know. And, of course, being married to a surgeon, I'll know what's needed here to . . . help Dr. Palmer get his practice established." She raised her eyebrows meaningfully and glanced at her daughter. "That is, as long as he insists upon burying himself here. Though I can't possibly see any future for Brent in this miserable place."

Kitty made a determined effort to ignore the snide comment, steering the subject to Christine's nursing degree. "Where did you train, Miss Westbrook?"

Christine mentioned a reputable hospital in Chicago, adding that she had gone into nursing at the urging of her physician father. "Frankly, it was a struggle, but I'm very persistent once I've tackled a project."

"And you've done beautifully, dear." Mrs. Westbrook snapped a lighter and ignited another cigarette, between puffs explaining to Kitty that her daughter was involved in too many social and charitable activities to tie herself down to a full-time job, especially since she didn't need to work. "But she's contributed her services to all sorts of worthwhile causes, raising funds for the hospital auxiliary's work and doing relief work on Fridays at the clinic. It's been a most rewarding investment of your time, hasn't it, dear?"

"Oh, yes," Christine said flatly.

"And, of course, it's been a good preparation for being married to a professional man," Mrs. Westbrook continued. "I've always maintained that being a doctor's wife practically requires an education in medical matters."

"Social matters," Christine said. "Be honest, Mother. You don't know the first thing about Daddy's practice, except for seeing to it that the right people consult him."

Mrs. Westbrook accepted that as a compliment. "You can't say it hasn't been important."

Christine laughed. "That sounds dreadfully snobbish, doesn't it, Miss Simmons? But a doctor's wife can determine the quality of his practice. Even in a small town like this, I suspect."

Kitty had exhausted her pretense of being busy at the desk. The Westbrook women were being amiable, if condescending, and it would have been rude to walk away from them without an excuse. The only one she could produce was her concern over Doc Osgood. "If you'll excuse me, I . . . have to check on Doc. He hasn't been well and he might want his lunch sent up to his room."

As Kitty began to escape, Mrs. Westbrook said, "I hope I'll be able to absorb all these peculiarities before we begin to change them! A hospital sending out for meals — a retired doctor living on the second floor." She laughed a tinny little laugh. "It's all so *absurd!*"

"It's *quaint,*" Christine corrected. "Mother, this is Brent's decision, and while it lasts we've got to be patient. He's terribly sensitive, and if we start ridiculing. . . ."

It was as though Kitty was not present. Either that, or the Westbrooks had no qualms about discussing their opinions in the presence of hirelings. "I am *not* going to behave like a mother-in-law, Christine, so please relax. I'm here as chaperone, and I can't think it will take Brent too long to realize he's made a mistake. Men can be stubborn, though. And I'm sure that if he expects you to stay in this dreary place until he comes to his senses, he won't object to my . . . perking this museum up a bit." Mrs. Westbrook rose majestically as Kitty neared the door. "It's no wonder there aren't any patients! I wouldn't have believed a waiting room could be this dismal!"

It used to be crowded with people who loved and needed Doc, Kitty thought. Kids came here and felt at home. The hospital was a friendly place to them . . . they weren't afraid to come here. And no one was ever hesitant about coming here for help. They'd leave a due bill for car repairs or a dressed turkey if they didn't have money, and they left with their health restored and their pride. We had all the patients we could care for, then. We didn't need the smug advice of a nurse who's never done any nursing or the wife of a rich "society doctor."

At the door, remembering that Eldridge and Doc's hospital probably were startling to city sophisticates (Brent had been appalled), Kitty swallowed her personal resentment and tried to emulate Doc's hospitable manner. She turned, addressing Mrs. Westbrook. "I hope you've enjoy your stay here," she said. "The Ritz is a little old-fashioned, but the rooms are clean and. . . ."

Mrs. Westbrook had started to laugh quietly, turning her face aside as though she were too polite to express open hilarity but couldn't help herself.

Unnerved, Kitty stammered, "Anyway, I hope you'll be comfortable." She gave way to a perverse instinct, adding, "As long as it lasts."

Her sarcasm was wasted on Christine and her mother. As Kitty started up the corridor, she heard a muffled giggling from both women, and then Mrs. Westbrook's *sotto voce* question, "Did she actually say 'The Ritz'? Oh, that's too funny! That is simply . . . *lud*icrous!"

Christine's voice followed Kitty down the hall, cautious and reproving: "Mother, *please!* You're going to make Brent so angry, he'll stick it out here just to spite you. And I'll die here. I'll simply *die!*"

Twelve

Christine Westbrook did not "die" in Eldridge. She masked her disgust with the town and her contempt for the hospital with a faked enthusiasm that Kitty might have applauded had the performance been given on a stage instead of in a loved institution.

During the next week, with the weather continuing oppressively hot and seemingless airless, Christine spent most of her time at the hospital, functioning not as a nurse but as a decorator. She functioned as an expert psychologist, too, preventing her mother from making in front of Brent the derogatory statements that were freely expressed in Kitty's presence.

"You'd think they wouldn't trust you with their opinions," Erma said one evening while Kitty was having dinner with the Danielsons.

"You mean they actually scheme about giving Dr. Palmer enough rope . . . expecting him to quit the hospital and go back to the city with them?"

"They not only talk about it, Christine makes chummy little comments to me about how silly men are and how you have to play along with their temporary whims." Kitty sighed. "She wouldn't take me into her confidence if she wasn't completely sure of herself."

George Danielson looked up from his steak with a quizzical expression. "You mean she doesn't think you're in her class, so that rules you out as a possible competitor. A lot she knows."

"Competitor?" Erma sounded shocked. "Kitty isn't even faintly interested in Dr. Palmer. George, what a ridiculous thing to say."

Erma's husband made a wry face and went on eating. Kitty had come to the same conclusion, but she regretted her slipup. No one in town except Vernon Olwyler knew that she was wracked with jealousy whenever Christine Westbrook breezed into the office and planted a kiss on Brent's cheek. Or called him "darling." Or sat holding hands with him across a table at Aunt Emma's. Unless she wanted to launch a Pity Poor Kitty club in Eldridge, no one else was going to know, Kitty decided. She was grateful when Erma brought the conversation back to the Westbrooks' manic redecorating program:

"If they don't think Dr. Palmer's going to stay, why are they tearing everything apart? I was in the church basement yesterday, pricing things for our rummage sale, when the older Rafferty boys brought in those lovely old wicker pieces. I wanted to cry. It was like . . . I don't know. It was like final proof that we don't have Doc's hospital any more." Erma's eyes had moistened. "I hear Mrs. Westbrook ordered plastic furniture from an office supply shop in St. Paul."

"As a gift for Brent," Kitty said. "It came yesterday. All new and shiny and . . . impersonal. The rolltop desk was put out into that shed at the back of Doc's property. And they're redoing Doc's old office now. I feel like a stranger there now."

"Wouldn't be so bad if you were busy," George muttered through a mouthful of salad. "I've been trying to get folks to see Dr. Palmer, but. . . ." He shrugged. "You know how people are."

"Do you mean to tell me Dr. Palmer just stands there and takes all that reshuffling?" Erma was indignant.

"He wanted to make changes himself," Kitty said.

"And he thinks new chairs are going to

bring people back?" Erma made a sniffing sound. "He's been here long enough to know better. Had enough problems without those two females around. I've had them in the drugstore a few times and they act like they're on a slumming tour."

Kitty nodded. "I know."

"Well, surely they can see that the hospital's gone to ruin," Erma persisted.

Kitty agreed with that statement, too. Christine and Mrs. Westbrook commented on the lack of patients whenever Brent was not in the room. He was miserably aware of it, too. His fiancée was right: only stubborn male pride was keeping him in Eldridge now, and it was only when she saw him apart from the Westbrooks that Kitty saw the look of utter defeat in Brent's eyes.

Erma forced another helping of mashed potatoes on Kitty and brightened. "Oh, well. I look for the whole shebang to move on before too long. Doc will find another doctor somewhere — though it's a shame, really. Dr. Palmer knew exactly what to do for my sister's migraine, and just look at the Rafferty boy. Good as new."

"I'd hate to see Brent Palmer leave," George said. He caught a deep breath. "Although, if we don't get a little breeze pretty soon I'm going to move out myself. This pressure-cooker weather gets me down!"

"Vernon was saying that very thing to me this morning," Erma said. She was bright and animated now that she had opened the doors to her favorite topic. "It's got to be pretty bad when Vernon complains. Have you ever met a more agreeable person? You never hear a negative word from him about anyone, and he really thinks the world of you, Kitty. He was telling me. . . ."

"Erma's off and running again." George grinned, winking at Kitty.

"She could do a lot worse than marrying Vernon Olwyler," Erma bristled. "At least she'd get some appreciation. Lord knows she isn't getting that at work. Not even from Doc."

It was true. On the contrary, the next afternoon, when Kitty felt driven out of the hospital by the two decorating demons, seeking refuge in Doc's study, he was far from sympathetic when she told him, "They've even taken your diploma and your license off the wall. Doc, isn't there something we can do?"

"You can stop trying to get my dander up, that's what you can do!" he growled. "I'd just as soon have my diploma up here. It doesn't mean anything downstairs, with me retired."

"It's just that. . . ."

"Just that you can't get it into your fool head that you aren't directing the hospital. Brent Palmer is. And if I'd ever asked a young lady to marry me, I would have expected her to fix my office up so's it was suitable. That girl's going to be the doctor's *wife*, Kitty. You've got no call findin' fault with what goes on downstairs."

Kitty stopped herself from mentioning the lack of patients; the reminder would have been too depressing for Doc. It would have disturbed him, too, to know that the new doctor's future wife was playing a waiting game — that she couldn't wait to get out of Eldridge and take Brent with her.

"Trouble with you," Doc went on, "you got spoiled, working for me. Too bossy. Telling me how to keep my books and what to wear on a rainy day. By golly, you can't do that with a sharp young doctor. And you sure aren't any match for those two . . ." Doc weighed his words for a second, "those two fireballs he's got on his side."

Later, seeing that Kitty was disconsolate, Doc turned on the blustering act with which he usually showed his affection, punching Kitty's arm playfully and saying, "I was the first person ever to smack your bottom, girl, and if I'd known you were going to grow up always complaining, I'd have whopped you twice." He lapsed into reverie after that, murmuring, "Twenty-two years ago. By golly, it seems like yesterday, and here you are makin' a fuss over some ratty old chairs I bought at an auction fifteen years before *that.*"

How could Doc be facetious, how could he stand aside and let strangers tear apart the rooms in which he had practiced his art for nearly half a century? Hadn't his first concern always been for the people of Eldridge, for their well-being? His practice had fallen apart in a few short weeks. Many of his "kids" — and these included just about everyone in town who hadn't seen fifty yet — were delaying medical care because the drive to the nearest medical facility was unpleasant during this stifling heat. Doc *had* to know that Mrs. Steele's husband had rushed her to West Fork in a wild, middle-of-the-night ride, only to have their baby born unattended, before they reached the out-of-town hospital. Doc knew. Didn't he care?

Kitty asked the question of Vernon Olwyler the next day, when the schoolteacher came to pay one of his almost daily calls on Doc. "He talks to you a lot," she said. "Hasn't Doc said *anything* about

140

what's happening?"

"About the only comment I've heard him make," Vernon replied, "is something to the effect that people who aren't getting good medical service in Eldridge are cheating themselves by choice. It's true Kitty. Doc saw to it that he was replaced by a good doctor. If people reject Dr. Palmer, there's nothing anyone can do about it."

"I would have thought it would break Doc's heart," Kitty said. "But it hasn't."

"Don't bet on it," Vernon told her. "What do any of us do when we're heartbroken and there's nothing at all that can be done about the situation?"

Kitty's eyes met Vernon's for a revealing instant. "We pretend that we don't care," she said.

"And we hang on, hoping for miracles."

No one could say whether or not Doc was following that course. But looking into herself, Kitty knew that this was all she was doing. Ironically, the man who's love she could not return, was "hanging on" and hoping for a miracle, too.

Thirteen

"It's got to break," people in Eldridge said about the weather, yet the sun beat down relentlessly on Main Street, and Kitty found it impossible to fill her lungs with the leaden air on that afternoon in late August when she walked back to the hospital after her lunch at Aunt Emma's. The ambulance truck had been driven away during her absence, Kitty noticed. Mrs. Westbrook's Cadillac sat in the driveway, behind Brent's sports car.

Kitty stepped into the waiting room and nearly ran into a large carton that had been placed near the doorway. Tim Rafferty and his mother were lugging a second carton down the hall.

"What's all this?" Kitty asked.

There was a disgusted expression on Mrs. Rafferty's usually pleasant face. Her flame-colored hair hung over her forehead in damp wisps. "You've never heard me complaining about hard work before, now, have you, Miss Simmons?" The second box was set down next to one of the new plastic chairs. "But when them two get on a rampage, they want everything done right now."

Kitty leaned down to open one of the cartons. "I know, but . . . what's . . . ?" At least a dozen packs of sterile cotton had been hastily piled on top of an assortment of sealed apothecary jars and boxes of bandages. Kitty looked up at the cleaning woman, aghast. "These are all the supplies from Doc's emergency cabinet!"

"Yeah, well, Mrs. Westbrook's had me clearing that out," Mrs. Rafferty said, mopping her forehead with the back of her wrist. "She says this is old trash that hasn't been looked at in years and it's just taking up good space. We're to take this stuff out to the shed."

"Of course it hasn't been used!" Kitty exploded. "It's an emergency supply! There's nothing here that isn't usable. Besides, it's not in anybody's way. There's nothing in that big storeroom except the cabinet and those folding beds. . . ."

"That's why I got Tim to come and help me," Mrs. Rafferty said. "I can't move all those cots out by myself, and that's what Mrs. Westbrook wants done. I said couldn't they wait until the truck gets here to take them over to the Community Center? But *she* says no, she wants to start measuring the room for all-over carpeting."

"All-over . . . ?"

"They want to fix the storeroom up for Dr. Palmer's new office," Tim explained. "I guess the other one's too small."

"But there's no window in the storeroom!" Kitty exclaimed.

"Going to install fluorescent lights and an air-conditioner," Mrs. Rafferty said. "Air-conditioning. That's what we need around here. Picked the hottest day of the year to start a job like this."

"Does Dr. Palmer know . . . ?"

"Don't ask me. He's gone out to see Hermit Joe, over next to our place. I told him Joe's been flat on his back two days now . . . slipped disk, looks to me. You ask *them* what they're doin'. I just work here."

Tim had opened the screen door to the porch. "I guess we can carry the beds out here for the time being, huh, Ma? They can't get a truck until four o'clock."

Mrs. Rafferty scowled at the cartons. "We sure as heck can't pile 'em up in here." She released a long sigh. "Well, let's start. No use wastin' time, bein' they're in such a hurry."

"Wait a minute!" Kitty intercepted Mrs.

Rafferty and her son as they started for the corridor. "Nobody's moving anything until Doc gives his okay." Furious, she pounded toward the back end of the building, too angry to wonder whether or not Brent had approved the move.

Christine and her mother, both smartly clad in slacks and sleeveless blouses, were coming out of the huge storeroom as Kitty neared the door.

"It's sweltering in there," Christine complained. "Mother, we can't possibly finish the room without Brent knowing about it. He's around most of the time, and when people come to install. . . ."

"But wouldn't it be lovely to surprise him?" Mrs. Westbrook cut in. "One day open the door and let him see his new office. . . ." She stopped talking as she noticed Kitty. "You'd keep our secret, wouldn't you, Miss Simmons? We're planning to clear out this wasted space and convert it to. . . ."

"It's not wasted space!" Kitty snapped. "It's where Doc keeps his emergency supplies!"

Mrs. Westbrook glanced at her daughter. "Well . . . really!"

Christine tried to be more affable, though she, too, had been startled by Kitty's angry tone. "Dr. Osgood's probably forgotten about all those creaky beds and things. I'm sure he doesn't even remember. . . ."

"He does, too, remember! There was a bus accident on the highway near here twelve years ago, and those cots were. . . ."

Mrs. Westbrook's sudden laugh was infuriating. "Only twelve years ago? I was hoping we'd discovered some genuine antiques. Really, my dear, you can carry sentiment just so far. I'm a doctor's wife, and I can certainly see the reason for emergency supplies, but there are enough beds in this building to accomodate all the patients Dr. Palmer's ever going to see. *Empty* beds, I might point out. And you'll agree that he deserves a more impressive office than that tiny hole in the wall that can't even accomodate the new furniture we've. . . ."

"If that office was good enough for Doc Osgood, it's good enough for anybody!" Kitty cried out. Resentment and jealousy had placed a final strain on her nerves, and, like the weather, something had to give. "Why don't you leave things alone? You aren't planning to stay in Eldridge. You've had nothing on your minds since you came here except getting Dr. Palmer to leave. You're playing games and ruining a hospital that Doc spent a lifetime building up." Somewhere behind Kitty a door closed. She whirled around to tell Mrs. Rafferty and Tim that the cots were not to be moved without Doc's approval. "This may be Dr. Palmer's *practice* — what's left of it — but everything in this building belongs to. . . ."

Kitty gasped, finding herself facing Brent. In almost the same instant she heard Doc's footsteps thumping down the stairway.

"There may not be anything left of my practice," Brent said icily. "But this is still a hospital. There's no excuse for anyone screaming like a fishwife in this corridor."

Kitty's face felt as though it were on fire. Charitably, Christine made an attempt to smooth over the ruckus. "We're just having a friendly little argument, darling. Miss Simmons doesn't quite see eye-to-eye with Mother on a. . . ."

". . . On a project that we'd hoped to keep as a surprise," Mrs. Westbrook said indignantly. "Brent, really, there is a limit to what you should tolerate from an employee. Every improvement we've tried to make. . . ."

"The waiting room's empty!" Kitty had burst into tears, and it no longer mattered that she was shouting or that Brent was staring at her, his expression more pained than hostile. "Doc had a *hospital* here, before you came!" Perversely, Kitty was ignoring Mrs. Westbrook and addressing her words to Brent. Accumulated frustration and long-suppressed envy demanded that Kitty strike out at someone, and, since the others meant nothing to her, Brent was the most likely target. "Don't you see what you've done? You'll go back to Chicago when these two operators decide to pull the strings. You'll go into a fancy practice, like your father-in-law. What you know won't count. Knowing the 'right people' — that's what'll matter." Kitty placed a scathing emphasis on "the right people," turning a scornful look at Mrs. Westbrook. "And you won't care that you've ruined Doc's hospital, wrecked. . . ."

"Kitty!"

She spun around at Doc's furious bellow.

"We don't talk to guests that way in this town. It's a damned cinch a nurse doesn't talk that way to a doctor!"

Kitty had never seen Doc angrier. "I'm thinking about *you*," she cried. "About your patients. You don't know. . . ."

"I know you're either going to get over this jealous streak of yours and learn to work with Dr. Palmer or. . . ."

Kitty's breath congealed inside her. This was Doc talking. *Her* Doc. The one person on earth she had always believed was firmly on her side, because she was on his. It was like fighting a common enemy and having your captain turn to attack you. Kitty lowered her head. "Or *what*, Doc?" she asked. Her voice broke. "If you mean what I think you do, I can be out of here in . . . ten minutes."

"Nobody wants you to leave, girl! I'm just telling you you've got to stop mixing your personal feelings into the way a doctor wants to run his practice. By golly, if I'd ever had a nurse in love with me, I'd have had a fine mess on my hands, now, wouldn't I? It's not anybody's fault the doctor's already got a wife picked out."

It was the coldest, cruelest blow imaginable. This humiliation before the three people who were staring at her in various degrees of superiority and disbelief was painful enough. But to have this humiliation come from Doc! This calloused, unfeeling revelation of a secret that had not even been entrusted to him . . . that had probably been passed along as a confidence by Vernon Olwyler. . . .

Mrs. Westbrook added the *coup de grace*. "Well. That may explain some of our difficulties, Christine!"

Kitty didn't wait to hear more. A wracking sob escaped her, and she covered her face with her hands, brushing past Brent Palmer and then past Doc, wanting only to run and hide. She felt four pairs of eyes following her embarrassed exit as she raced for the tiny room in which her spare uniforms and oxfords were kept. When she reached the dark privacy of that room, pulling the door closed behind her, she sank to a wooden bench and wept like a lost child.

Fourteen

Kitty had packed her few possessions into a carton, delaying the process and dreading the moment when she would have to emerge from the airless cubicle in which she had exhausted her supply of tears. Carrying the box of uniforms and shoes through the building on her way to the hotel would mean risking an encounter with Brent. She couldn't bear to face him. Worse, she hadn't the strength to face Christine or Mrs. Westbrook. Their smug or pitying expressions when they glimpsed her swollen red eyelids would add insult to injury. Yet she couldn't sit in this steam-bath of a room all day.

Then there was Doc. Leave without saying good-bye to him? The thought seemed incredible. Still, to part with Doc, feeling that he was no longer a friend who could be trusted. . . . Wouldn't it be better to remember him as a father, protector, beloved physician, the crude old saint who had never before inflicted an intentional hurt?

Tears were threatening Kitty again as she weighed her decision. She shifted her thoughts to more practical matters. A bus left for West Fork from in front of The Ritz at seven that evening. From there she could make connections for . . . where? Any city. It didn't matter. She would have time to pack her things at the hotel, pay a final call on George and Erma Danielson, close her tiny account at the bank, and . . . what else? What else did you do when you closed the door forever on the only place where you truly belonged?

A knock on the door startled Kitty. She got to her feet hurriedly, hoping the powder she had daubed on would conceal the blotches around her eyes. She opened the door to see Brent standing in the corridor. He seemed too agitated to notice Kitty's appearance or her embarrassment.

A quick glance over Kitty's shoulder told the doctor what she had been doing. "Were you leaving?" Brent asked.

Kitty avoided his eyes. "Yes."

"I'm afraid you'll be safer here," he said. "Besides, I may need you, Kitty. If it hits anywhere near Eldridge. . . ."

Kitty forgot her personal anguish. "If what hits? What's wrong?" She emerged from the sultry confinement of the small room to see Tim Rafferty racing up the hallway from Brent's office.

"The announcer just said it cut right through the downtown section," Tim announced. "The radio's cracklin' so bad we can't hardly hear, but it looks like the West Fork movie house was right in the path. Cars blown around like they was feathers, the guy said. And the hospital. . . ."

"The hospital?" Brent threw a shocked glance at Kitty. "My God, a few minutes ago we heard they were moving people to the hospital from. . . ." Brent turned to Kitty. "A twister demolished a trailer park on the outskirts of West Fork."

Suddenly there was pandemonium. A waitress rushed in to report that she'd seen the devastation on TV at Aunt Emma's and that there was scattered cyclone activity reported from other nearby areas. Everyone was gathered around the radio in Brent's office by then, and it was Doc who looked out the window and saw the ominous black funnel on the horizon.

"My kids!" Mrs. Rafferty screamed. "I've got to get to my kids. . . ."

Kitty pictured the flimsy shack on the edge of Indian Rock Canyon; there were no storm cellars in that remote area, and a blow would send the house flying over the

153

precipice as though it were a cardboard toy. "I'll go get Mike and the others," she said.

"And Joe . . . Hermit Joe," Tim Rafferty remembered. "He can't even get outta bed."

"We may both be needed here," Brent said tersely. He looked around the room quickly, waving down Doc's offer to go — Mrs. Rafferty didn't know how to drive; Christine was a nurse and might be needed. His eyes rested on Mrs. Westbrook. "Lucille . . . if Timmy here, shows you the way. . . ."

Mrs. Westbrook only blanched. It was Christine who replied, "Brent, you *aren't* asking Mother to go out into some God-forsaken place with the threat of a cyclone . . . ?"

Brent didn't answer. His facial muscles rigid, he turned to Tim. "Let's go, son." Perhaps he was excusing the Westbrooks' cowardice when he added, "You'd need help getting Joe into the truck, anyway. We won't be gone long."

The phone was ringing, and Brent waited while Kitty answered a desperate call from the police chief in West Fork. She dropped the receiver, reporting, "They're sending four badly injured people here by ambulance. The whole north wing of the hospital is rubble, and they're without electricity."

154

Grim, Brent looked out at the dark moving column threatening Eldridge. "Get the extra beds set up. Watch that funnel, and get everybody here into the storm cellar if it gets any closer. I'll be back as fast as I can." As he started into the corridor, Brent nearly tripped over a carton that had been removed from the emergency supply room. "If this is what I think it is," he ordered, "get it unpacked. I want first aid supplies where we can get at them in every room. *Stat!*"

The last order was barked at Christine and her mother. Kitty, Doc, and Mrs. Rafferty had already started the process of preparing the hospital for emergency care.

"You aren't going to leave us here?" Mrs. Westbrook demanded. Her eyes bulged with terror at the second black shape that had materialized, frighteningly near the town. "Brent, we've got to get out of here while we can. Christine. . . ."

Christine's panic was more acute than her mother's. "Honey, don't go! We can find out which road is the safest and. . . ." Her fear turned to anger under Brent's icy glare. "You dragged us into this pesthole. It's been horrible enough, but now that our lives are in danger, you're running out on us!"

"I'm doing what I came here to do," Brent said. "I'll appreciate whatever help I can get."

155

"If you leave. . . ." Christine was following Brent down the hall, hurrying to catch up with his determined stride. She was on the verge of hysteria, groping for a threat strong enough to stop Brent. "You won't find me here when you get back. Mother and I are leaving! You won't see me again!"

Brent was out of Kitty's view as she carried the carton of emergency supplies into one of the examining rooms; the only response she heard was the sound of his rapidly accelerating footsteps. From the waiting room, she heard a thumping sound, as though Brent had kicked into one of the chairs. "Get this junk out of the way and get the room cleared — we may need to set up cots in here. And *unpack these cartons!* Who in hell moved a carton of bandages out *here* in the first place?"

A door slammed, and seconds later the Chevy truck raced off, the roar of its motor all but drowned out by Christine's hysterical sobs. "We can't stay here! Mother . . . what are we going to do?"

The waitress from Aunt Emma's and Mrs. Rafferty were sliding collapsed folding beds out of the storeroom, with Doc instructing them as to where they should be set up. As Christine and her mother held a shrill conference about their escape, Doc broke the tension that had gripped the hospital. Incredibly calm, his eyes twinkling with a perverse amusement, he thumped one of his huge hands against Mrs. Westbrook's back. "You could run over to the cellar at the community hall, but you might get tired of the company. Every old checker player in town is down there by now."

Mrs. Westbrook tossed Doc a murderous look.

"Best bet is to stay right here," Doc said. He yelled a few instructions at Kitty, answered a question from the waitress who was volunteering her services, and waved a greeting as Vernon Olwyler came hurrying through the waiting room, followed by a veritable army of his upper-grade students.

"I figured you might need help," Vernon said. "Looks bad, doesn't it?"

Doc turned his back on the Westbrooks until Vernon and the youngsters had been put to work setting up beds. The women were on their way out of the building as Doc called out, "I'm serious, folks. This is the only solid brick building in town. It ain't pretty for nice, but it's hell for stout. You don't want to be out somewhere on the highway if. . . ."

Christine shouted something about the black funnels moving in an opposite direction from the Southeast Highway, and then they were gone. Kitty was too busy to watch their departure. Mrs. Rafferty, concerned about her children, made periodic trips to the porch, watching the course of the twisters. It was she who noted, "My stars, those women didn't even stop at The Ritz for all their fancy clothes. Silliest thing — drivin' off like that, when everybody knows this is the safest place around."

"Might be the busiest, too," Doc observed quietly. He had been standing near a window, studying the skyline in the direction of Indian Rock Canyon. Then, seeing the apprehension in Mrs. Rafferty's face, he tried to lighten the suspenseful mood. "That so-called nurse had a hunch she might be called on to do a little honest work. I think that sent her out of here as fast as being worried about her own hide."

Mrs. Rafferty made a distasteful smirk. "You think they're gone for good?"

Surprisingly, Doc walked over to where Kitty was laying out an emergency pack and patted her shoulder. "Well, we can hope so, can't we, girl?"

Kitty frowned. "I had the impression you were pretty sold on the Westbrooks. You took me over the coals for trying to stop them from getting rid of our emergency supplies. There's a truck coming at four o'clock to haul off all those beds we're setting up. Did you know that?"

The radio, which had gone dead, came back on with a crackle of static, and Mrs. Rafferty hurried to the office to hear the latest reports.

"I know you were burned up about *some*thing," Doc said. "Here, let me take a couple of these packs across the hall."

"Don't run away," Kitty said.

Doc stopped in the doorway, sheepish. "If you're going to raise Cain with me because I let Brent know how you feel about him. . . ."

"It wasn't like you, Doc. To . . . humiliate me. I . . . wanted to die."

"By golly, I was beginning to think you'd already done that, girl. Good-looking woman who's got so much in common with a struggling young doctor . . . seems to me you'd have had sense enough to let him know you were on his side. I figured *somebody'd* better tell him." Doc shrugged. "So I did."

"But the way you. . . ."

"I did it *my* way," Doc said.

Bluntly, openly, honestly. Kitty gulped back the threat of a fresh deluge of tears. "Oh, Doc, you . . . I thought I'd lost my best. . . ."

"Your best friend? You better believe it." Doc's arms opened up to clasp Kitty close to him as she ran across the room. "*One* of your best friends, sweetheart. By golly, if Vernon hadn't told me why you turned him down, I wouldn't have guessed. The way you started out nagging Brent and complaining about him. . . ."

"I *love* him, Doc!" Kitty let the big arms hold her in a tight, fatherly embrace. "I'm so scared. I . . . look out there! I didn't want him to go, either."

"But you knew why he was going, didn't you, Kitty? And you let him go. Do you think he's such an oaf that he can't separate the women from the girls?" Doc held Kitty for another second, then pushed her away abruptly. "Okay, that's enough mush for one day. We've got patients on the way. Let's move!"

It was a thrill to hear Doc sounding like his old self, bawling orders at everyone in the hospital — telling Mrs. Rafferty to "stop acting like a damn worry-wart" and yelling at Vernon Olwyler that it was a good thing he knew how to teach school, because he'd never make the grade as an orderly. His raucous manner relieved the suspense; he kept everyone too busy to notice that, outside, the air was deathly still, yet heavy with the threat of the screaming whirlwinds that had demolished most of another hospital nearby.

"Sure is good to have Doc in charge again," Mrs. Rafferty said.

For her sentimental loyalty, she got a verbal drubbing from Doc: *"I am most certainly not in charge! I'm only filling in until the head of this hospital gets back!"*

The head of the hospital got back in what seemed like a span of years — but in what had probably been the fastest run between Indian Rock Canyon and Eldridge in history. Mrs. Rafferty took time to hug her redhaired offspring, but Kitty was forced to control her own joy at seeing Brent safely returned. Hermit Joe, immobilized by back pains and disoriented in the strange surroundings, required medication and a sympathetic ear. Kitty was occupied with him when the first two patients from West Fork were carried in by ambulance attendants. She was helping Brent, and Doc gave emergency care to the more seriously injured of the pair — a man who had suffered multiple fractures and a deep head laceration, when the shrill wind cry penetrated the operating room. The eerie whistling noise was followed by a muffled rumbling and the sound of agitated young voices outside the door.

Brent looked up at Kitty over the operating table, and Doc muttered, "That was close," but there was no interruption in their teamwork effort. When their sedated patient had been settled in a hospital bed across the corridor, they had only moments to hear that a twister had ripped through a block-wide area of the east end of Eldridge, shattering the community hall and tearing the roofs from a row of houses in its path. The swath cut by the ferocious wind left its toll of victims behind; by late afternoon, when the news announcer broadcast an all-clear weather report, every bed in Doc's hospital was occupied, and patients needing minor attention crowded the waiting room and porch.

There was no time for conversation; Kitty moved mechanically, responding to Brent's orders — sometimes anticipating them, but rarely leaving his side. And the hospital was suddenly filled with more than patients. Volunteers streamed in to offer their services: Eldridge's overalls-clad mayor, trained in civil defense during World War II, found himself in charge of the blood bank. Housewives became nurses, bank clerks served as orderlies. Aunt Emma's kitchen was staffed by the town's best cooks, with Vernon's juvenile nature-club members acting as delivery boys.

It was a miracle of organization out of chaos, mostly undirected; people saw what needed to be done and did it. With a steady parade of contusions, fractures, and lacerations to tend to, Brent Palmer had no time to question the orthodoxy of accepting amateur help. By eleven that night, when the last patient requiring minor care had been treated and released and the seven more seriously injured victims were resting quietly, he joined Doc, Vernon Olwyler, and Kitty in his office for coffee. He looked exhausted and bedraggled, but his dark eyes shone with satisfaction; there were no patients whose recovery would not be complete.

Sighing, Brent sank to the edge of a modern bench that had replaced Doc's old black leather sofa. "This thing sits like a lumber pile," he grunted.

Doc was tired, too, but he laughed. "You're beginning to sound like me, fella."

Kitty nodded her agreement as she served Brent's coffee. "That's what a lot of people kept saying today."

Brent scowled, but he was interested. "They said that about me?"

"Well, by golly, you were racing around, yelling and cussing whenever you needed something." Doc helped himself to a slice of apple pie from the display of homemade pastries that had accumulated on the desk. "I *guess* you sounded like me. Everybody hopped to. Must have been nerve-racking for you . . . all those people running around."

Brent stared at the floor for a few seconds. Then he looked up at Doc. "I don't know what we'd have done without them, Doc. Or without your planning. If we hadn't had emergency supplies. . . ." He shook his head, his expression telling Doc and Kitty that whatever the hospital had lacked in modern decor it had made up in preparedness.

Vernon had been on his feet all day, but he got up now to offer a plate of sandwiches to Brent. "The concensus seems to be that you're even *tougher* than Doc Osgood, Dr. Palmer. I heard that from a highly authoritative source."

Brent helped himself to a ham on rye. "Who's that?"

"Nettie Craig."

Doc looked startled. "I didn't see her here. She wasn't hurt?"

"Her chauffeur got a shoulder bruise from flying timber," Kitty explained. "The old girl brought him in personally."

"I think she got a good look at Dr. Palmer in action while she was here," Vernon said.

164

"Anyway, she came back with these about an hour ago." He thumbed at the sandwiches.

"Peace offering," Doc muttered. He leaned back in the plastic chair that was too small for him and closed his eyes. He had taxed his strength far beyond its capacity, but he looked rested suddenly.

They finished their coffee in silence, and then Brent got to his feet. "Doc, you get to bed. That's an order."

Doc grinned and moved to obey. Vernon helped him out of the snug chair. "Tell me what I can do, Dr. Palmer, and. . . ."

"No, you've done enough. Kitty and I will manage." Brent held a brief discussion with Kitty regarding medication for one of the patients from West Fork, and the quartet moved out into the corridor.

"I'd certainly be happy to stay," Vernon insisted. "You're both tired and — it's really too much for just one doctor and one nurse."

"He's going to need another nurse, all right," Doc said. "With folks coming back and . . . for a while, Brent, you're going to have to take care of people from West Fork. Maybe *you* can work around the clock, but Kitty. . . ."

Vernon hadn't been around when Christine and Mrs. Westbrook had fled, and there hadn't been time to tell him about their departure. "You know, it's been so hectic, I hadn't noticed. But . . . didn't you *have* another nurse here, Dr. Palmer?"

Brent stared into space for a second. "No," he said. "No, I didn't, really." He said goodnight to Doc, thanked Vernon for his help, and turned to Kitty. "Let's have another look at the Maxton boy. I want to be sure he's properly gorked for the night."

It was a typically "Doc-ian" phrase, and Kitty reacted with an exhausted grin. She waved goodnight to Doc and to Vernon, then hurried to keep up with Brent's quick stride up the corridor.

The hall lights were dim at this hour, and she may only have imagined it, but it seemed to her that as Vernon turned toward the waiting room on his way out he winked at her.

Fifteen

"I know you won't like this," Kitty said, "but I can't keep telling the accountant that we're too busy to get our books in order."

Brent pulled one of the wicker chairs closer to the rolltop desk. Nobody questioned Mrs. Rafferty about how she had managed to retrieve the wicker pieces; two days ago, when the last of the cyclone victims had been released, the old furniture had somehow reappeared, along with Doc's framed diploma, which now hung in its old place on the reception room wall beside that of Brent Palmer, M.D.

It was past eight P.M., though the street lights had not yet been turned on along Main Street. A rosy afterglow lingered on after the sunset; a faint breeze hinted at the nippy fall days to come. "We may as well get it over with," Brent said. "We're not expecting anyone else, are we?"

"No appointments," Kitty told him. "Although. . . ." She thought for a moment. "I saw Mr. Vandermeer at the café, and he said he might come in this evening and have you look at that ingrown toenail. Depending on whether he gets his garage roof finished, he said."

"That's what I like. Precise hours."

Kitty looked to see if the doctor was annoyed or if he was merely being facetious. It was impossible to tell. Cautiously, she opened the bookkeeping ledger into which she had been scribbling notations all week. "As I said, you aren't going to like this. I thought I'd better ask about . . . some of these . . . accounts payable."

"I thought we'd agreed to let an accountant handle the books," Brent said. There was no doubt about it now; he sounded irritated.

"Yes, but you have to approve some of these deals." Hesitantly, almost fearfully, Kitty scanned the current sheet. Brent had not made any drastic changes around the hospital since the near-tragic cyclone had swept through Eldridge. He had given grudging approval when the Rafferty boys replaced the old black leather couch in his office. But, then, he hadn't retracted his disapproval of the haphazard appointment schedule or of Doc's old method of accepting nonnegotiable fees.

Of course he had been too busy with patients to devote any time to reform measures. His acceptance by the community had delighted Kitty, but, disappointingly, Brent had not changed his politely impersonal attitude toward her. There had only been one note of encouragement in recent days: The letter that had arrived for Brent bearing Christine Westbrook's name and return address had been dropped into the office wastebasket minutes after Brent had given it a hasty reading. To Kitty's knowledge, it had not been answered.

Still, it was too much to hope that Brent's warmer relationship with the citizens of Eldridge had changed his attitude toward efficiency. The figures before her seemed ludicrous even to Kitty. "There's Carl Maxton's bill for his boy. He's the mechanic from West Fork, and . . . well, he can pay part cash now, but he said if you want the Chevy overhauled, he'd give it a thorough going over. It . . . does need a new carburetor."

Brent's face was impassive. Kitty went on, feeling less comfortable, reading off a list of "normal" accounts and then taking a deep breath as she came to a series of long scribbled notes. "I don't know what you can do about Hermit Joe if you don't like goat cheese, Doctor. That's all he can offer, and I'll pay his bill myself before I'll offend him. I . . . took the liberty of saying you liked goat cheese just fine. And the Carpenters — they're the newlyweds who rent my house . . . you remember . . . you put seven stitches over his right eye — well, he's just gone back to work after a month's layoff, and they're expecting a baby. Peggy's got an appointment for a prenatal exam tomorrow, but she's still working at Aunt Emma's, and Emma wondered, since the kids aren't exactly flush right now, if she could work it out so that part of what we owe her for meals could be applied to. . . ." Kitty stopped to reread the complicated financial proposition made by the café's owner during lunch. "Maybe I didn't remember it right. We owe the restaurant . . . no, let's see: If Emma gives Peggy the raise she wants to give her, but doesn't tell her about it, and deducts that money from what we owe *her*. . . ."

It sounded absurd, and Kitty colored under the intense stare that Brent was beaming at her. Suddenly, embarrassed by her own confusion, Kitty slammed the book shut and cried, "I'm not a bookkeeper, I'm a *nurse!* This is the way Doc would have worked it out. But you're not Doc, and . . . I don't have the right to ask you to . . . do

170

things his way. I. . . ." Kitty got to her feet. "I don't even know what to do about Mrs. Craig's check. If I send it back, she'll. . . ."

"Don't send it back."

Kitty turned to see that Brent had gotten out of his chair, too, and was standing inches away from her. He was laughing quietly and shaking his head back and forth in that now-familiar incredulous manner. "I wish you'd go on — I've needed a good laugh. I was hoping you'd get to something really crazy, like gooseberry preserves or . . . well, I guess goat cheese *is* pretty funny."

"It's not funny to these people," Kitty said. "It's the difference between keeping their pride and losing it. As Doc says, you have to learn to accept as well as to give. You. . . ."

"Deposit Mrs. Craig's check," Brent said. He was solemn now, his eyes riveted to Kitty's.

She paused, not sure she had understood him correctly. "It's a . . . *big* check, Doctor. I'm afraid to tell you how much, but . . . it's enough to buy the orthopedic equipment we need and to — well, Mrs. Craig's note said we might want to hire a couple of practical nurses if we can't get an R.N. There's enough to pay salaries for the year."

Brent nodded. "Doc told me she was

going to do that. Partly her way of saying she's sorry, and partly — the way she explained it to Doc — because she wants to enjoy seeing the money spent while she's still around. It's going to be willed to the hospital, anyway."

"I . . . don't want to tell you what to do," Kitty said. She felt perilously close to tears. "I've done that too much, and I'm sorry. And . . . look, I wouldn't blame you if you gave up on this crazy town. You aren't *ever* going to bring it into the jet age. The people here. . . ."

"Are rather wonderful, when you give them a chance," Brent said. He sounded too much like Vernon Olwyler to be true. But any doubts that might have sprung into Kitty's mind were erased as Brent added, "I didn't come here to change them, Kitty. I came because I'm a doctor . . . I wanted to serve them. They've had to give in a little and . . . I've had a lot to learn. But they've started paying me the greatest compliment I could have hoped for, Kitty. They're saying I'm a lot like Doc." Brent glanced at the ledger that Kitty had set on the desk. "They're even paying my fees 'Doc-fashion.' It's very rewarding. It's more than I deserved."

"Doc couldn't have done more for them

than you're doing," Kitty said. "You're . . . a lot like him, Brent."

His hands had reached out to grip Kitty's shoulders. "More than you know. Doc loves you, girl." Brent's eyes looked deeply into hers for a prolonged, electrifying moment. "How do I say this? By golly, it took me long enough to realize this, but . . . I love you, too. I never really loved a woman before. I love you enough to . . . replace the comic book library out here. Enough to want you to *marry* me."

She was in his arms, clinging to Brent as he kissed her — tenderly at first and then with a consuming passion. They held each other close for a long while — making up for lost time, and somehow, between kisses, blueprinting the plan for perpetuating Doc Osgood's dream and creating one of their own.

"Mrs. Brent Palmer . . . Mrs. Brent Palmer!" Kitty was rehearsing the unbelievable words in her mind silently, excitedly, when the reception room door opened and Brent released her from his embrace abruptly. They were both flustered and breathing hard as they greeted the limping patient who had come in.

"Got my roof back up," Mr. Vandermeer said, pretending that he had noticed nothing unusual. "So I figured I'll hobble on by and see can you have a look at this blasted toe. That is, if you got the time right now, Doc. Otherwise, I could come by, say, between noon and two o'clock to-morrow. . . ."

"I've got the time now," Brent said. He dismissed Kitty with a formal nod. "I won't need you for this, Nurse. I imagine you have something you want to do."

Kitty mimicked his grave professional manner. "Yes, doctor. I have to make a re-port."

"Make it fast," Brent said. "It shouldn't take me long to operate if I don't bother with an anaesthetic." He waited to see Mr. Vandermeer's horrified expression, then let out a roar of laughter as the patient realized he was being ribbed.

Kitty heard them both laughing as they walked up the corridor to the nearest exam-ining room, but the sound was lost in her rush to the stairway. She had climbed the steps to Doc's living quarters many times before — and usually in a hurry. But this was the first time, Kitty thought, that her feet would not have to touch the steps: When you had a beautiful miracle to report, wasn't it logical to fly?

We hope you have enjoyed this Large Print book. Other Thorndike Press or Chivers Press Large Print books are available at your library or directly from the publishers.

For more information about current and upcoming titles, please call or write, without obligation, to:

Thorndike Press
P.O. Box 159
Thorndike, Maine 04986 USA
Tel. (800) 223-1244
    (800) 223-6121

OR

Chivers Press Limited
Windsor Bridge Road
Bath BA2 3AX
England
Tel. (0225) 335336

All our Large Print titles are designed for easy reading, and all our books are made to last.